SONIC X

by Diana G. Gallagher

Spaceship Blue Typhoon

Grosset & Dunlap

GROSSET & DUNLAP
Published by the Penguin Group
Penguin Group (USA) Inc., 375 Hudson Street, New York, New York 10014, U.S.A.
Penguin Group (Canada), 10 Alcorn Avenue, Toronto, Ontario, Canada M4V 3B2
(a division of Pearson Penguin Canada Inc.)
Penguin Books Ltd, 80 Strand, London WC2R 0RL, England
Penguin Ireland, 25 St Stephen's Green, Dublin 2, Ireland
(a division of Penguin Books Ltd)
Penguin Group (Australia), 250 Camberwell Road, Camberwell, Victoria 3124, Australia
(a division of Pearson Australia Group Pty Ltd)
Penguin Books India Pvt Ltd, 11 Community Centre, Panchsheel Park, New Delhi – 110 017, India
Penguin Group (NZ), Cnr Airborne and Rosedale Roads, Albany, Auckland 1310, New Zealand
(a division of Pearson New Zealand Ltd)
Penguin Books (South Africa) (Pty) Ltd, 24 Sturdee Avenue, Rosebank,
Johannesburg 2196, South Africa

Penguin Books Ltd, Registered Offices:
80 Strand, London WC2R 0RL, England

Used under license by Penguin Young Readers Group. Published in 2005 by Grosset & Dunlap, a division of Penguin Young Readers Group, 345 Hudson Street, New York, New York 10014. GROSSET & DUNLAP is a trademark of Penguin Group (USA) Inc. Printed in the U.S.A.

Library of Congress Cataloging-in-Publication Data

Gallagher, Diana G.
  Spaceship Blue Typhoon / by Diana G. Gallagher.
     p. cm.
  Based on an episode of the television program Sonic X.
  ISBN 0-448-43997-2
  I. Sonic X (Television program) II. Title.
  PZ7.G13543Spa 2005
  [Fic]—dc22
                        2005010363

10 9 8 7 6 5 4 3 2 1

The Big Small Mistake

Chris Thorndyke stood in the transport pod. He had started to build it after Sonic left Earth. That was six years ago!

"This is dangerous," Chris said. "But I want to see Sonic again."

The pod glowed. The light covered Chris. Everything went dark and quiet. Then he saw the light coming from the Master Emerald.

Sonic and his friends looked surprised.

"I did it!" Chris exclaimed. "I'm in Sonic's world!"

"Sonic!" Chris started to run, but he tripped and fell. His shirt and pants were too big!

"Chris, long time no see," Tails said.

"How are you?" Cream asked.

"Your clothes are too big!" Sonic says to Chris

"I shrank!" said Chris. He was eighteen when he left Earth, but on Sonic's planet he was back to the size of a twelve-year-old. "I think there was a problem during the teleportation."

"How'd you get here?" Amy poked Chris.

"I built my own transmission pod," Chris said with pride.

"Who is he?" Cosmo asked Sonic.

"A friend." Sonic gave a thumbs-up. "Hi, Chris!"

Cheese jumped on Sonic's head.

"Sonic!" Chris grinned. "You haven't changed at all!"

"You look the same, too," Sonic said. "But your clothes are too big."

Chris agreed. He'd only been twelve when Sonic left Earth!

"I'm not *quite* the same," Chris started to explain. Then he gasped.

Sonic gave Chris a friendly slap on the back. "Well, we're glad you made it anyway."

Then he fell facedown on the ground.

A Terrible Tale

"Sonic passed out," Tails said.

"He just needs to rest." Cream's mother tucked Sonic into Cream's bed.

Chris hitched up his baggy pants. He went back into the living room. Everyone was listening to Cosmo.

"Those **monster robots** are called Metarex," Cosmo said.

"Metarex," Amy said.

"Many planets have been attacked by the Metarex." Cosmo looked worried. "No one in outer space is safe."

"Metarex want to rule the universe," Cosmo explained. "They will fight to have total order."

Chris pictured the terrible things Cosmo told them. The Metarex destroyed everything!

Cities were bombed. People screamed and ran. Mountains exploded. Forests burned. Trains and airplanes crashed.

"They have conquered many planets," Cosmo said.

Chris imagined an army of monster robots.

"The Planet Egg holds the world's life energy," Cosmo said. "The Metarex take the Planet Egg away."

Chris pictured a planet. The planet cracked and the Planet Egg burst out. A robot grabbed the Egg!

"Nothing can live on a world that has lost its Planet Egg," said Cosmo.

Chris pictured a world like Earth. It was blue and white. It turned brown and got smaller. Then it vanished! He saw other planets blink out one by one.

"Could that happen to *this* planet?" Amy asked.

Cosmo nodded.

"Why do you know so much about the Metarex, Cosmo?" Knuckles crossed his arms. "Did you bring those robots here?"

Cosmo looked shocked. "The Metarex have no heart! I'm not like them at all!"

"Why should we trust you?" Knuckles asked.

"My people are gone," Cosmo said. "But Sonic uses the Chaos Emeralds. He can stop the Metarex and save the universe."

Chris left the living room with Tails and Amy. Cosmo was crying. She really had come to ask Sonic for help.

"It sounds bad," Chris said.

Amy nodded. "You came just in time to help, Chris."

"And you built that pod in just six months," said Tails. "Amazing!"

"No, six *years* have passed on Earth," Chris said. "I'm eighteen."

"What?" Amy and Tails looked at each other.

Amy and Tails are surprised by Chris's size

"You're awfully small," Amy told Chris. **"I was tall, but I shrunk,"** Chris said. "There was a problem when I **teleported."**

"A *big* problem," Tails said.

"I can't change that now." Chris shrugged. "But I'm sure I can fix the problem eventually."

Amy opened Cream's bedroom door and stopped. "Sonic!"

The bed inside the room was empty. Sonic was **gone!**

Dark Day, One Hope

Chris, Amy, and Tails ran into the bedroom.

"Sonic is gone!" Tails cried.

Chris walked over to the bedroom window. "It's open."

Amy stared at the empty bed. "He ran away."

"He takes off when he gets well," Tails said. "Sonic just can't sit still."

Chris smiled. "He hasn't changed at all."

Sonic ran superfast. He looked like a blue wind going in and out of the trees.

He sped through the green forest.

Sonic zoomed up a hill and ran into the mountains. He stopped on the edge of a cliff and looked down.

Chris, Cream, and Amy watch as Sonic speeds away

"What?" Sonic gasped.

Everything below him had changed.

The trees were brown. All the leaves were burned off. The lake was almost dry. The ground was cracked.

Sonic's world was dying!

Cosmo stood in Cream's yard watching through the bedroom window as Cream's mother gave Chris a shirt that fit.

"What do you think of our planet?" Cream asked Cosmo as they played in the yard. "Do you like it?"

"I do like it." Cosmo looked back at the house. Amy brought Chris a cup of tea. Tails gave him cookies.

"I don't want the Metarex to hurt your world," Cosmo said. She vowed to protect the planet.

Cream smiled. "We have Sonic, so we'll be fine."

"But the Chaos Emeralds are gone," Cosmo

"It's my fault the Chaos Emeralds are lost"

said. "Sonic needs them to beat the Metarex."

A blue blur whizzed in. Sonic stopped between Cream and Cosmo. "Then we have to find the Chaos Emeralds."

"Sonic!" Cosmo was surprised to see him.

"It's my fault the Chaos Emeralds are lost," Sonic said.

Sonic told Cosmo about his fight with Dark Oak.

He described how Dark Oak had raised a sword. "Just hand the Chaos Emeralds over!"

Sonic was weak, and he knew there was only one way to keep the emeralds safe. "Chaos Control!" he said, flinging the emeralds into outer space.

The emeralds went in all directions. The light from them blinked out. They were all lost in space.

Dark Oak would not be able to get the Chaos Emeralds now.

Sonic had grinned. Then he'd fallen toward his home world.

"I couldn't beat Dark Oak," Sonic said.

"But you can beat the Metarex," Cosmo said.

"Don't worry." Sonic raised his hand. "We'll get the Chaos Emeralds back. We'll beat the Metarex and save the Planet Egg!"

"Let's go look for the Chaos Emeralds!" Amy exclaimed.

"It will be a great adventure!" Cream added.

"Maybe fate brought me here to help," Chris said.

"We need a spaceship," Tails said.

"Okay!" Sonic grinned. "We're off to outer space!"

Power Plays

Everyone followed Tails down to his work-shop. They stopped on the landing.

"It will take months to build a spaceship," Chris said.

"Oh, just wait and see." Tails pushed a switch.

A large motor **roared.** Bright lights came on. Sonic whistled. There was a huge machine in the basement!

"This is the Blue Typhoon," Tails said. "We have a spaceship. But we need the Chaos Emeralds for power."

Chris noticed the Master Emerald sitting on its altar. "Use that!"

Chris and Sonic put the Master Emerald in

the **Blue Typhoon**, as Amy, Cream, Cosmo, and Cheese watched.

"Looks good!" Tails called.

"Hey!" Knuckles ran in. He stopped by the group under the ship. "What are you doing?" Knuckles was the guardian of the Master Emerald. He felt very protective of it.

"Just borrowing the Master Emerald," Sonic said.

"We're all going to outer space," Amy explained.

"Outer space!" Knuckles looked surprised.

"We're going to find the Chaos Emeralds," Cosmo said. "We need them to stop the Metarex."

"We need your help, too, Knuckles," Cream said.

Knuckles frowned. "I want the Master Emerald back."

Cosmo gasped. "But the whole universe is in **danger!**"

Cosmo, Cream, and Amy surrounded Knuckles.

"Hey, hold it!" Knuckles exclaimed. "Help!"

"When it comes to angry girls, there's no winning." Sonic grinned.

There was much to do before the Blue Typhoon could take off.

Knuckles carried steel frames. Amy brought snacks.

Tails showed a diagram to Sonic. "The Master Emerald's power goes into the energy chamber."

Sonic nodded. "All right."

Then Tails went to the bridge. "I'm sorry this happened just when you got here, Chris."

"No problem." Chris sat at a computer. "I can help. The flying program is done."

"I'll tell Knuckles to test the startup," Tails said.

"Next, let's put in some superdevices," Chris said.

"Sounds great!" Tails grinned.

Both computer screens hissed with static.

Metarex Spike passed by a satellite in space. The robot's eye flashed.

Chris and Sonic install the Master Emerald

"Hey, hold it!"
Knuckles exclaims

"Do not let them finish that spaceship!" Dark Oak's voice boomed. "Do not let it take off!"

Metarex Spike turned and sped toward the planet.

Metarex
Spike
Attacks

Amy and Cream walked up a hill. They carried packages and wore backpacks filled with food.

"Tails will get the water we need," Amy said. "We'll put the food on the spaceship."

"Then we'll be able to **take off.**" Cream was excited.

Cosmo sat on a rock at the top of the hill. She looked worried and sad.

Cream set her packages on the ground. "Do you want to help us carry these, Cosmo?"

"Sure!" Cosmo lifted the packages. They were heavy, and she stumbled.

"Are you all right, Cosmo?" Cream asked.

"I'll be fine." Cosmo started walking. She

tripped and fell down the hill. Apples and cans rolled everywhere.

"Cosmo!" Cream and Amy ran after her.

"Are you hurt?" Amy asked.

"I don't think so." Cosmo started to get up. The heavens turned dark for a second. A gust of wind blew past. Something fell from the sky. An **exploston** boomed near Tails's workshop!

"That's the Metarex!" Cosmo pointed toward the mountain.

The monster robot changed its shape as it stood up.

"For the sake of order!" the Metarex exclaimed. "I will fight anyone that tries to stop me!"

The **robot shot beams from its fingers.** The beams missed the workshop.

"Adjusting aim," the robot said. It fired again.

A blue wind zoomed in! Sonic hit the Metarex in the head.

The beams missed the workshop again.

Sonic jumped and kicked the giant robot.

"Phooey!"

The Metarex started to fall.

Knuckles flew in. He grabbed the robot's head and pushed the Metarex into the ground.

Sonic ran over to look.

Knuckles landed beside him.

The dust cleared. The Metarex was buried in the ground.

The robot moved its finger. Then a sword appeared. The Metarex grabbed the sword.

Sonic and Knuckles jumped when the Metarex swung the sword.

Knuckles landed in the clearing. "An ordinary attack won't stop this thing."

Sonic looked at Knuckles. "But we have to try!"

The Metarex stood up. It was ready to attack again. "I cannot let you leave this planet!"

The Metarex shoots beams
from its fingers

Almost Launch Time

"Is that the Metarex?" Chris asked. He watched the huge robot through the window.

"It found out about our spaceship," Tails said.

"How are we doing?" Chris asked.

Tails looked at the computer screens. "Most of the ship is ready. We can work on the rest while we're flying."

Chris agreed.

"Will you get Knuckles, Amy?" Tails talked into his wrist communicator. "We have to  the Master Emerald."

"Okay, Tails." Amy clicked off her communicator. "Cream, tell Knuckles to go back to the ship."

"What's going on?" Cosmo asked.

Sonic and Knuckles
face the Metarex

Knuckles pounds the robot on the head

"Tails wants to take off soon!" Amy explained.

"I'd better hurry!" Cream ran to find Knuckles.

Sonic watched the robot from the top of a tree.

The Metarex dropped the sword. Its fingers glowed. It aimed to fire more beams.

"**Hiyaaaah!**" Knuckles pounded the robot on the head.

The ground smoked where the Metarex fell. The robot got up. Then it stopped moving.

"What's the matter?" Knuckles asked the robot.

Thorns flew out of the robot's chest!

"Look out, Knuckles!" Sonic yelled.

Sonic and Knuckles ducked and jumped. All the thorns missed. But they were headed for the spaceship!

On board the ship, Tails turned a key on the bridge. "Engine activated!"

Then Tails saw the thorns on the computer screen.

The thorns came closer and closer.

A blue blur zoomed in. Sonic hit all the thorns

away. They fell to the ground and exploded.

"A hedgehog can't get stung by thorns," Sonic said. "It would be too embarrassing!"

The Metarex shot another beam from its fingers. The beam hit behind the workshop. Then the robot tilted!

Knuckles dug up the ground all around the Metarex.

A hole opened under the robot.

The Metarex fell in.

Knuckles looked down. "I hope you learned your lesson!"

"Knuckles!" Cream ran up with Cheese. "Come right away! Tails wants to take off!"

A sword came out of the robot's hand. The Metarex swung.

Knuckles jumped out of the way.

Sonic sped down from above. He hit the Metarex in the head. "Go, Knuckles! I'll take care of things here!"

Cream, Cheese, and Knuckles ran.

Sonic turned to face the angry robot.

Countdown

Amy stacked packages in the spaceship.

Cosmo carried Cream's backpack into the cargo room.

"We have to load as much food as we can," Amy said. There were piles of supplies outside.

"Okay." Cosmo turned to get more. She lost her balance and fell.

"You're pushing yourself too hard, Cosmo," Amy said.

Tails sat on the bridge. He pushed two switches. The panel beeped. The yellow light turned on.

"Systems are go!" Tails raised a lever.

"Main engine connected! Ignition!"

"Main engine connected," Chris said in the engine room. He raised a lever.

Knuckles chanted. The Master Emerald glowed.

Chris lowered another lever. The main engine groaned and started up. "We have ignition!"

"Mother!" Cream ran into her house. "May I stay over at Tails's place?"

"On that spaceship?" Cream's mother asked. "Sure, but don't get in the way."

"I won't." Cream hugged her mother. It was hard to leave her.

Sonic fought the Metarex in the forest. He jumped up and hit the robot's face.

The Metarex swung at Sonic.

Sonic stopped the punch with his hands and legs. He came back with a kick. "Yah!"

The robot stopped Sonic's kick. It circled and landed. Then the Metarex looked toward the workshop.

"We have ignition!"

The ground cracks
More rocks fall

"Tails?" Sonic called out to warn his friend.

The rocks around the workshop started to fall.

"More thrust," Tails said from inside the Blue Typhoon's cockpit.

The power indicator on the computer screen got longer.

"11.6 million tons of horsepower!" Tails said. "Ready to take off!"

The ground around the workshop cracked. More rocks fell.

Sonic could see part of the spaceship.

"I won't let you leave!" the Metarex said, puffing out its chest.

It fired ten thorns.

Sonic jumped when the thorns flew. "Oh, no you don't!"

The ground fell away from the Blue Typhoon.

Sonic chased the thorns at top speed. He destroyed six thorns.

Four other thorns zoomed toward the spaceship.

Sonic went speeding after them. He knocked the thorns away one by one.

The Metarex stood tall in the forest.

Sonic landed on the edge of the Blue Typhoon. He glared at the robot. "I won't let you touch our spaceship!"

Sonic
vs.
the Metarex

Knuckles raised his hands. "Master Emerald, **lend me your powers!**"

The Master Emerald lit up the engine room.

"Seventy, eighty, ninety," Chris said. "Energy supply is full!"

The Metarex moved toward the spaceship.

Tails spoke through the speaker. "Sonic! Let's use the main cannon! Stand by!"

The trees beside the Blue Typhoon fell. The cannon appeared.

"Move **energy** from the chamber into the cannon!" Tails told Chris.

Chris redirected the energy flow.

"Energy is in the cannon tube," Chris said.

Sonic ran past the cannon.

"Start your spin, Sonic!" Chris yelled.

"Okay!" Sonic shouted. He spun faster and faster.

The Metarex landed in front of the spaceship.

Amy stored the last package in the cargo room.

Cosmo, Cream, and Cheese looked tired.

Chris's voice came over the speaker. "Everyone get ready for a shock!"

The Metarex changed outside the spaceship. Thorns appeared in its chest.

"Trigger safety off!" Tails called. He set the cannon. "Target Metarex ahead."

The Metarex fired its thorns.

Chris and Knuckles ran onto the bridge.

"Sonic, fire!" Tails yelled.

A spark lit inside the cannon. Light blazed. Sonic shot out and knocked away the thorns.

The Metarex stood to attack again.

Sonic rammed right through the giant robot.

The Metarex lands in front of the spaceship

The Metarex fires its thorns

A hole appeared in the Metarex. It exploded.
Then Sonic spun away into the sky!

Spaceships Away

The spaceship Blue Typhoon broke free of the rocks.

Sonic could not stop spinning as he fell through outer space back toward the planet.

"Sonic!" Chris flew up in the Hyper-Tornade, a souped-up version of the X-Tornade.

"Chris?" Sonic opened his eyes.

The Hyper-Tornade closed in. The cockpit opened.

Chris stood with his arms wide. He grabbed Sonic's hand and pulled him into the Hyper-Tornade.

"Sonic recovery complete," Chris

radioed Tails.

"Roger!" Tails sat on the bridge. "Here goes."

The main cannon went back into the spaceship.

"Main wing open!" Tails exclaimed. "Spaceship Blue Typhoon take-off!"

The engine flamed. The Hyper-Tornade docked.

Amy, Cosmo, Cream, and Cheese waited in the cargo room.

"Let's go to the bridge!" Amy said.

"Yes!" Everyone ran out behind Amy.

And the Blue Typhoon rose into the sky.

Sonic, Chris, and Tails looked out the front window.

Amy, Cosmo, Cream, and Cheese ran onto the bridge. They all walked over to the window.

Sonic scratched his head. He felt something funny. He pulled out a wire. "Who put this micro-phone on me?" Sonic asked.

Decoe sat in the cockpit of the Egg Crimson. He looked at Eggman. "Sonic found the bug."

Sonic finds the bug

Eggman laughed. "Okay, then. We'll take off, too."

"Roger!" Becoe grabbed a lever. He lowered it. The engines fired on.

"Engine ignition!" Bokkun yelled. "Egg Crimson take-off!"

"Huh!" Eggman frowned at Bokkun. "How dare you say that? I'm supposed to give the launch orders!"

Then Eggman's spaceship, Egg Crimson, chased after the Blue Typhoon, and the battle for the Chaos Emeralds continued.

Egg Crimson takes off

Ingleborough: Landscape and history

by David Johnson

Pages: 288, softback & hardback
Illustrations: 100 photos and diagrams
Page size: 246 × 189mm
Hardback ISBN: 978-1-85936-187-0
Softback ISBN: 978-1-85936-188-7
Price: Hard, £25; soft £14.95

Ingleborough: Landscape and History presents new, ground-breaking research in several areas – geology, geomorphology, archaeology and history – all presented in a way which will appeal to visitors and local people alike. The book is profusely illustrated with photographs and illustrations.

Few books relate the biography of a mountain. This new book – perhaps the most comprehensive and well researched of the genre – does just that for one of the best-loved, most historically important and interesting hills in England. Published by local publisher, Carnegie, in association with the Yorkshire Dales Millennium Trust, Ingleborough will appeal to everyone who loves the Yorkshire Dales and the great fells of northern England.

"...clearly organised and engagingly and lucidly written, well-referenced and illustrated with crisp maps and diagrams and a large number of colour photographs."
G.C.F Forster, Northern History 47(1)

"...this book is a tour de force...It combines scholarship and extensive original research with a highly readable narrative style, as accessible to the general reader as the specialist geologist or landscape historian."
Colin Speakman, Yorkshire Dales Review 105 (2009)

*Historic Walks
in & around
York*

Historic Walks
in & around York

25 leisurely city & country rambles

Brian Conduit

First published in 2011
by Palatine Books,
Carnegie House,
Chatsworth Road
Lancaster LA1 4SL
www.carnegiepublishing.com

British Library Cataloguing-in-Publication data
A catalogue record for this book is available from the British Library

Printed and bound in the UK by Halstan Printing Group, Amersham

ISBN: 978 1 874181 74 3

Contents

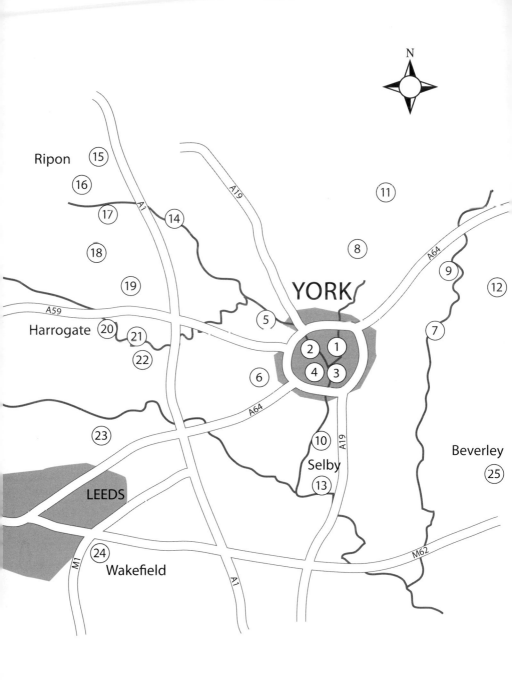

N

Ripon (15)

(16)

(17) A1 (14)

(18)

(19)

A59

Harrogate (20) (21)

(22)

(23)

LEEDS

(24)
Wakefield

A19

(11)

YORK

8

A64

9

12

5

2 1

4 3

6

A64

7

10

Selby

13

Beverley

(25)

M62

Introduction to York & the surrounding area

By any criteria York ranks as one of the great historic cities of Europe and is deservedly one of the most visited in Britain. Its range of attractions exceeds that of all other British cities, with the exception of London. It possesses England's largest and one of its finest medieval cathedrals, a castle, the ruins of a formerly great abbey, an almost complete circuit of medieval walls and a vast array of museums. The latter include major attractions of national significance, such as the Jorvik Viking Centre, National Railway Museum and Castle Museum, plus smaller local and regional museums, among which are the Yorkshire Museum, Merchant Adventurers' Hall, Fairfax House, Treasurer's House, Guildhall, Roman Bath House and many more.

But it is not just the major attractions that make York so uniquely interesting and appealing. There are fascinating old narrow, winding streets to explore, a large collection of medieval churches – some of which are half-hidden away and you come upon them unexpectedly – attractive green open spaces and pleasant riverside paths. The medieval walls and their four gates (called bars) are one of the city's greatest amenities and from the wall walk which covers most of the circuit – just over 4.8 km (3 miles) in length – you can enjoy bird's eye views of the city, dominated inevitably by the great bulk of the minster. Incidentally in the older parts of York the streets are called gates and the gates are called bars, a legacy from the Viking era.

The capital of the North

For centuries – until the rise of the great Industrial Revolution giants of Manchester, Sheffield and Leeds – York was the largest city in the north of England and regarded as the traditional capital of the North. It began its life as the Roman fort of *Eboracum*, remains of which lie under the minster. In the centuries that followed the collapse of Roman power in Britain, it became the capital of the Anglo-Saxon kingdom of Northumbria and the seat of one of only two archbishops in England, which has made it the religious capital of the north of England ever since. For a time it was the centre of a Viking kingdom that traded extensively with Scandinavia. After the Norman Conquest, a castle was established here and the minster was rebuilt. For much of the Middle Ages it was a target for Scottish raids, hence the constant updating of its walls. It suffered its last siege during the Civil War and in the more settled times of the eighteenth century it developed into a fashionable social centre. The nineteenth century brought the railways and York became a major railway centre, hence its choice as the location of the National Railway Museum. Nowadays it is a foremost international tourist attraction attracting visitors from all over the world.

In addition to the history, architecture, museums and visual attractions, there are hotels and guest houses of all sizes and price ranges, together with a superb and varied selection of restaurants, pubs, wine bars and cafés in which to relax while sightseeing.

Strolling around the streets and along the walls of this historic city, enjoying its sights and absorbing its unique atmosphere, is a pleasurable and rewarding experience, but

York is also a walking and tourist centre for the surrounding region. Beyond the city limits lies an attractive landscape which is threaded by a profusion of tempting and well-signed public footpaths. York lies at the heart of a fertile vale through which flows the River Ouse and its various tributaries – Ure, Nidd, Wharfe, Aire and Derwent. The walking here is mainly flat, leisurely and undemanding. Fringing the Vale of York are the Howardian Hills to the north, the chalk slopes of the Yorkshire Wolds to the east and the eastern edge of the Pennines, the backbone of England, and the Yorkshire Dales to the west. Within this area the range of historic attractions includes the Roman site at Aldborough, the superb monastic remains at Fountains and Kirkstall, the great churches at Selby, Ripon and Beverley, medieval castles and manor houses at Knaresborough, Sheriff Hutton and Spofforth, the deserted village at Wharram Percy, battle sites at Stamford Bridge, Boroughbridge, Wakefield and Marston Moor, the elegant Victorian spa town of Harrogate, and imposing country houses at Ripley, Beningbrough, Castle Howard and Harewood.

Combining visits to places of historic interest with walking through the winding streets of the city or along attractive country footpaths adds interest and variety to your walks and provides a new perspective on our history, enabling you to see the life of the castle, abbey, battlefield or country house unfolding before your eyes and to put the building or site in its geographical context. Enjoy both the walks themselves and the various historic places, take your time – none of the walks is lengthy – and why not add to the pleasure by popping into one of the many cosy old pubs or tea shops that are scattered throughout the area.

Useful addresses

The Ramblers' Association, Second Floor Camelford House, 87-90 Albert Embankment, London SE1 7TW Tel: 020 7339 8500 Email: ramblers@ramblers.org.uk

The National Trust, PO Box 39, Warrington WA5 7WD Tel: 0844 800 1895 Email: enquiries@nationaltrust.org.uk

Yorkshire Regional Office, 27 Tadcaster Road, Dringhouses, York YO24 1GG Tel: 01904 702021

English Heritage, 1 Waterhouse Square, 138-142 Holborn, London EC1N 2ST Email: customers@english-heritage.org.uk

Yorkshire and the Humber Regional Office, 37 Tanner Row, York YO1 6WP Tel: 01904 601901 Email: yorkshire@english-heritage.org.uk

Local tourist information centres

Beverley	0844 811 2070	beverley.tic@vhey.co.uk
Boroughbridge	01423 323 373	tip@boroughbridge.org.uk
Harrogate	01423 537 300	tic@harrogate.gov.uk
Knaresborough	01423 866 886	kntic@harrogate.gov.uk
Leeds	0113 242 5242	tourinfo@leeds.gov.uk
Malton	01653 600 048	maltontic@btconnect.gov.uk
Ripon	01765 604 625	ripontic@harrogate.gov.uk
Selby	01757 212 181	selby@ytbtic.co.uk
York	01904 550 099	info@visityork.org

Public transport

For information about bus and train services and timetables contact Traveline either by visiting www.traveline.org.uk or phoning 0871 200 2233. Alternatively contact the local tourist information centre.

The walks

The sketch maps are only a rough guide and you should always take with you an Ordnance Survey (O.S.) map. The best maps for walkers are the Explorer maps and the number and title of the relevant ones are given in the introductory information for each route.

Times given for the walks are approximate and are based on walking at an average speed of around 2 miles per hour with a few stops. The whole point of these walks is to take your time, enjoy the experience, stop for refreshment breaks or to take in a view and to visit the various historic places that are featured. This will add to the time, especially on the town walks in York itself where there are places to stop at and visit literally every few yards.

Visiting historic sites

Some of the historic buildings and sites featured in the walks are open all year round and are free to visit but most have restricted opening times and charge an entrance fee. In particular some English Heritage properties and most stately homes are closed during the winter months, approximately from the end of October to around Easter time.

In order to avoid disappointment, it is always best to enquire about opening times by contacting either the individual site or the nearest tourist information centre. The relevant phone numbers and email addresses for the latter are provided.

Key to maps

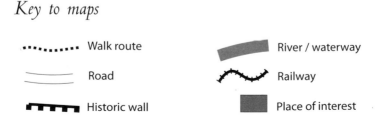

•••••••••• Walk route	River / waterway
—— Road	Railway
Historic wall	Place of interest

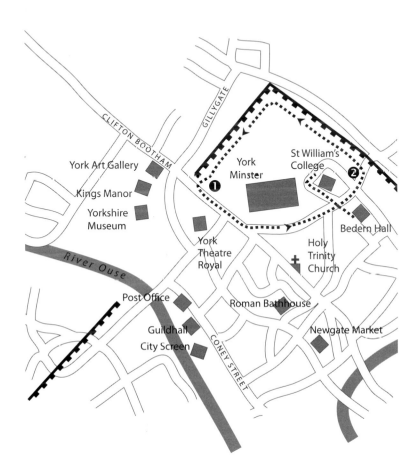

WALK 1

York: Minster & northern walls

....

LENGTH:	1.6 km (1 mile)
TIME:	1 hour
TERRAIN:	Easy town walking along streets and on part of the walls
START/PARKING:	York, Bootham Bar, GR SE602523. Car parks in York or alternatively use the Park and Ride scheme
BUS/TRAIN:	York is easily reached by train and bus from all the local towns
REFRESHMENTS:	Plenty of restaurants, wine bars, pubs and cafés in York
MAP:	*OS Explorer 290 – York*, or pick up a street map from the tourist information centre

....

The magnificent minster, the largest medieval church in Britain, is the focal point of this short walk. It also takes in the church where Guy Fawkes was baptised, the elegant Treasurer's House, St William's College and two of York's original four medieval gateways into the city, Bootham Bar and Monk Bar. On the stretch of the walls between the two bars there are superb views of the north and west sides of the minster, as well as some of the imposing houses and gardens adjoining it.

🛈 Bootham Bar, the entrance into the city from the north west, was built on the site of a Roman gateway. York ranks as one of the finest walled towns in Europe and its circuit of walls is the longest and one of the most complete in the country. It is also the only walled town in England that retains its four main medieval gateways, which are all called bars: Bootham, Monk, Walmgate and Micklegate. The Romans built the original defensive walls but these were rebuilt and considerably extended in the thirteenth and fourteenth centuries to protect the city, principally from the Scots. They were nearly demolished in the early nineteenth century but fortunately were saved and parts later restored by the Victorians. Apart from three brief gaps, the whole circuit can be walked and provides you with a succession of fine elevated views across the city.

🕴 ❶ **Pass through Bootham Bar and walk along High Petergate to the west front of York Minster.**

🛈 Looking up at the majestic west front of York Minster is a great experience. It was founded in 627 and stands on the site of the Roman headquarters building, some of the remains of which can be seen underneath the central tower. Since Anglo-Saxon times there has been a succession of churches on the site; the present building was begun in the early thirteenth century and not completed until the building of the massive central tower in the fifteenth century. Everything is on a massive scale, the minster is the largest medieval church in England and one of the largest in Europe, and the central tower is the largest in the country. The scale is immediately conveyed when you enter the church and walk down the awesome nave. Make a point of looking at the windows, as York Minster has more of its original medieval stained glass than any other cathedral in England.

West front of York Minster

ⓘ The minster has had its share of problems and catastrophes. It was damaged by fire in 1829 and then again in 1840. The most recent disaster was a fire in 1984 which destroyed the roof of the south transept. Take your time when looking around as you are visiting what is by any standards one of the great buildings of Europe.

🚶 **Continue along the south side of the minster along Minster Yard, passing to the left of St Michael le Belfrey church, and continue past a Roman column and the statue of Constantine the Great, bearing gradually left around the east end of the minster.**

ⓘ The present church of St Michael le Belfrey is a sixteenth-century rebuilding of an earlier church on the site. It is particularly notable as the church in which the notorious gunpowder plotter Guy Fawkes was baptised on 16 April 1570. A short distance away in High Petergate is the house in which he was born. It is now a hotel and inn and serves such interesting-sounding delicacies as Fawkes Fiery Sausages!

South side of York Minster

Opposite: Statue of Constantine the Great

Treasurer's House

(🚶) Just before reaching St William's College, make a short detour to the left along College Street and turn first right into Chapter House Street to the Treasurer's House.

ℹ️ Not surprisingly ghost stories abound among the narrow streets and ancient buildings of York, and both the Treasurer's House and St William's College have their share of these.

The Treasurer's House is so called because it was originally the home of the treasurers at the nearby minster. The present elegant building dates mainly from the seventeenth and eighteenth centuries, but after falling into a state of disrepair it was fully restored in the early twentieth century by a local industrialist called Francis Green. It has an attractive and secluded garden. The ghosts, allegedly seen by a plumber when working in the cellars, were a group of Roman soldiers looking unusually weary, dejected and scruffy as they marched along. Were they the ghosts of the Ninth Legion that was based in York and mysteriously disappeared without trace?

The fine, timbered St William's College was founded in the middle years of the fifteenth century as a college for priests from the minster. By the Victorian era it had become a slum but, like the Treasurer's House, it was restored by Francis Green. It is reputedly haunted by a seventeenth-century murderer. Both buildings are now restaurants.

(🚶) Return to College Street, walk past St William's College, go under an arch and turn left along Goodramgate to Monk Bar.

ℹ️ Monk Bar was the gateway into the city from the north east. Nowadays it houses a small museum to Richard III who had estates and castles in Yorkshire and, despite his generally bad reputation, enjoyed considerable popularity in the local area.

(🚶) ❷ **On the left side of the gate, go through a door, climb steps and at the top turn left along the wall. Follow the wall around a left bend to Bootham Bar where you descend to street level.**

Monk Bar

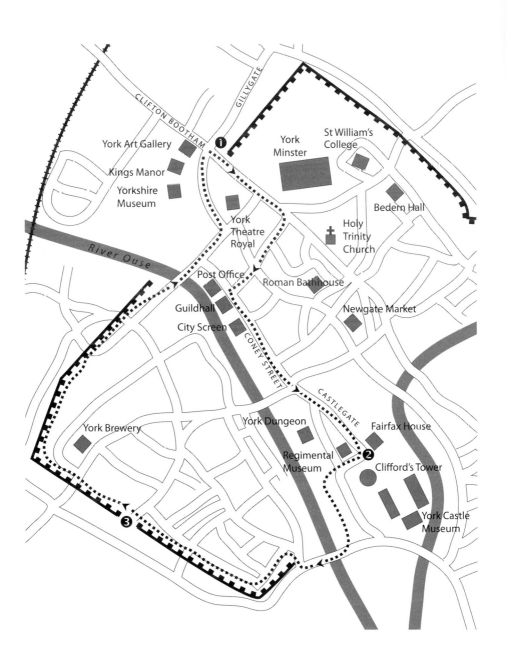

York Art Gallery

Kings Manor

Yorkshire Museum

CLIFTON BOOTHAM

GILLYGATE

❶

York Minster

St William's College

Bedern Hall

York Theatre Royal

Holy Trinity Church

River Ouse

Post Office

Roman Bathhouse

Guildhall

City Screen

CONEY STREET

Newgate Market

CASTLEGATE

York Brewery

York Dungeon

Regimental Museum

Fairfax House

❷

Clifford's Tower

❸

York Castle Museum

WALK 2

York: castle area & southern walls

....

LENGTH:	4 km (2.5 miles)
TIME:	1.5 hours
TERRAIN:	Easy town walking along streets, riverside paths and on part of the walls
START/PARKING:	York, Bootham Bar, GR SE602523. Car parks in York or alternatively use the Park and Ride scheme
BUS/ TRAIN:	York is easily reached by train and bus from all the local towns
REFRESHMENTS:	Plenty of restaurants, wine bars, pubs and cafés in York
MAP:	OS Explorer 290 – York, or pick up a street map from the tourist information centre

....

This walk takes you along the less-frequented part of the medieval walls on the south side of the River Ouse and towards the end you enjoy superb views over the city, dominated inevitably by the great bulk of the minster. Among the places of interest passed on the route are the Mansion House, Guildhall, Fairfax House and the complex of buildings and museums that make up York Castle. There is also a short stretch beside the river.

Mansion House

(🚶) ❶ **Pass through Bootham Bar and walk along High Petergate. In front of the minster keep ahead (still along High Petergate), turn right into Stonegate and walk down it into St Helen's Square.**

ℹ Stonegate is built on the line of the Via Praetoria, one of the main streets of the Roman city of *Eboracum*. Facing you as Stonegate opens out into St Helen's Square is the early eighteenth-century Mansion House. This handsome building is the official residence of the Lord Mayor of York and houses the civic regalia plus a collection of silver, furniture and paintings.

Behind the Mansion House and overlooking the River Ouse is the Guildhall, originally the meeting place of the city guilds. It was built in the fifteenth century but had to be almost entirely rebuilt after its destruction during an air raid in 1942. The interior is now used as a council chamber and meeting place for various committees. The best view of it is from the river, seen near the end of the walk when crossing Lendal Bridge.

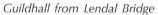 **Turn left in front of the Mansion House along Coney Street, keep ahead at a crossroads and where the road forks, bear slightly left along Castlegate to the castle complex.**

Guildhall from Lendal Bridge

Micklegate Bar – the entry into the medieval city from the south

ⓘ Just before reaching the castle you pass Fairfax House on the left. This grand Georgian town house was built in 1762 by John Carr, a renowned York architect, for Anne Fairfax, only daughter of Viscount Fairfax. Inside you can see some eighteenth-century furniture and an extensive collection of clocks.

The first castle at York was built soon after 1066 by William the Conqueror. In fact he built two, both of them originally wooden, this one and another on the opposite side of the River Ouse. The second one, which had a brief life, was never rebuilt in stone and occupied Baile Hill, which you later ascend to get onto the wall just after crossing the river. This first castle was of the basic motte and bailey design but the only remaining building is Clifford's Tower on top of the motte which dates from the thirteenth to fourteenth centuries. The former bailey

Clifford's Tower, all that is left of York's medieval castle

is occupied by a group of three eighteenth-century buildings, two of which make up the Castle Museum. You need to devote a lot of time to this museum – there are reconstructed Victorian streets, shops and rooms which give a vivid insight into the lives of people in the past, plus displays of old weapons, clothing, toys, utensils of various kinds and much more. One of the buildings was previously used as a prison and you can see the cell in which the notorious highwayman Dick Turpin was kept prior to his execution in 1739.

🚶 **❷ In front of Clifford's Tower turn right along Tower Street, keep ahead at a crossroads down Peckitt Street to the River Ouse and descend steps onto a riverside promenade. Turn left and the path continues through Tower Gardens (the first public gardens in the city) to Skeldergate Bridge. Climb steps beside the bridge up to a road, turn right to cross the bridge, take the first road on the right and immediately climb steps onto the wall. This stretch of the wall runs across part of Baile Hill. From here follow the wall as it bends right to Micklegate Bar.**

❶ Micklegate Bar was the entrance into the medieval city from London and the south. As the main gateway, it was frequently used to display the severed heads of traitors, ranging from rebellious medieval barons to Jacobite supporters of Bonnie Prince Charlie in 1746.

🚶 **❸ Continue along the wall as it bends right again (there are grand views of the minster from here) and eventually you descend to the road at Lendal Bridge. Cross the bridge, keep ahead along Museum Street and turn left into St Leonard's Place to return to Bootham Bar.**

Baile Hill, the site of York's second castle

Grand views over the city and minster from the walls

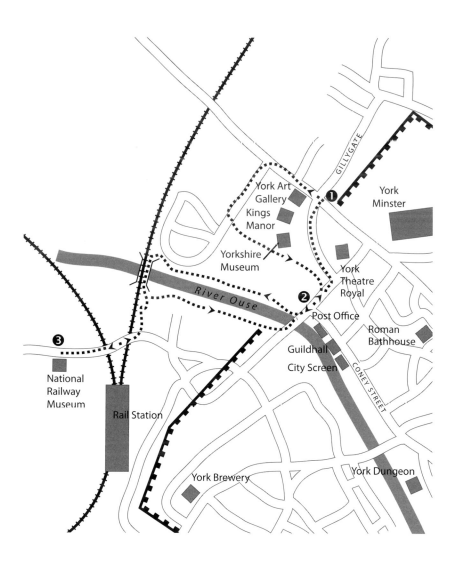

York Art Gallery

Kings Manor

Yorkshire Museum

GILLYGATE

York Minster

York Theatre Royal

Post Office

Roman Bathhouse

River Ouse

Guildhall

City Screen

CONEY STREET

National Railway Museum

Rail Station

York Brewery

York Dungeon

❶ ❷ ❸

WALK 3

York: museum gardens, River Ouse & National Railway Museum

LENGTH: 3.2 km (2 miles)

TIME: 1 hour

TERRAIN: Easy town walking on tarmac paths

START/PARKING: York, Bootham Bar, GR SE602523. Car parks in York or alternatively use the Park and Ride scheme

BUS/TRAIN: York is easily reached by train and bus from all the local towns

REFRESHMENTS: Plenty of restaurants, wine bars, pubs and cafés in York

MAP: *OS Explorer 290 – York*, or pick up a street map from the tourist information centre

This is the only one of the four walks within the city of York that is entirely outside the circuit of the medieval walls. It begins with a tour of the beautiful Museum Gardens, studded not only with colourful floral displays but also with a museum, the remains of a great medieval abbey and a Roman tower, part of York's Roman fortifications. You then continue along the east bank of the River Ouse and cross the river by a footbridge to visit the National Railway Museum. The return takes you along the west bank of the river.

Remains of the defensive wall around the precincts of St Mary's Abbey

(✖) ❶ **With your back to Bootham Bar, walk along the street ahead – called Bootham – beside part of the defensive wall that surrounded St Mary's Abbey. Take the first road on the left (Marygate), still by the abbey wall, and after passing St Olave's church, turn left through the former monastic gatehouse into the Museum Gardens, laid out in the early nineteenth century.**

❶ To the left are the ruins of St Mary's Abbey. The little survives, mainly parts of the north side and west end of the church, gives some indication of the scale and magnificence of what was the largest and wealthiest monastery in the north of England. Originally founded in 1055, it was refounded as a Benedictine abbey by William II in 1088 and most of the scant remains date from a thirteenth-century rebuilding. It was dissolved by Henry VIII in 1539.

Nearby is the Yorkshire Museum, built in 1830 and housing an extensive collection of archaeological finds and treasures from the Roman, Saxon, Viking and medieval periods. To the right is the Hospitium, the former abbey guest house. Although extensively restored, much of

Ruins of St Mary's Abbey

the ground floor dates back to the fourteenth century. Nowadays it is used as a conference and exhibition centre.

A little further on you pass to the right of the Multangular Tower. This impressive structure dates from around the beginning of the third century and was one of the corner towers of the original walls built around the Roman fort of *Eboracum*.

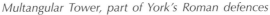 **At a fork take the left-hand path, passing the Roman Multangular Tower on the left, and keep ahead to exit the gardens. Turn right towards Lendal Bridge, do not cross it but turn right down steps, at a footpath sign Riverside Walk, to the River Ouse by Lendal Tower.**

Multangular Tower, part of York's Roman defences

❶ Lendal Tower was built around 1300 to defend the river crossing. Originally it was one of a pair and at times of danger a chain could be stretched across the Ouse to a similar structure, Barker Tower, on the opposite bank.

⊛ ❷ **Turn right along the riverside promenade as far as a railway bridge, climb steps in front of it and turn left to cross a footbridge adjoining the railway bridge. On the other side, turn left but almost immediately turn right, at a sign to the National Railway Museum. Walk along a path to a road, turn right, pass under a railway bridge and continue along Leeman Road to the National Railway Museum.**

❶ For many boys – and perhaps even more their dads – the National Railway Museum must be their idea of heaven. It opened in 1975 and houses a vast collection of locomotives, rolling stock including royal carriages, and railway memorabilia of all kinds. Among the latter are documentary film and old railway posters. The museum, the largest of its kind in the world, covers the entire history of the railways and, not surprisingly, is a major attraction.

⊛ ❸ **Retrace your steps to the river and turn right to follow the west bank back to Lendal Bridge, passing to the left of the War Memorial Gardens. In front of an arch of the bridge and just before reaching a road, turn right up steps and turn left to cross the bridge. Keep ahead along Museum Street towards the minster and turn left into St Leonard's Place to return to the start.**

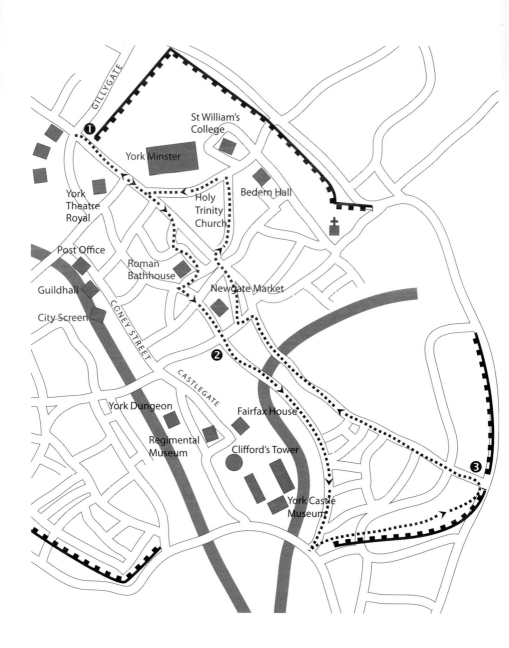

WALK 4

York: Jorvik, eastern walls & the Shambles

••

LENGTH:	4.8 km (3 miles)
TIME:	1.5 hours
TERRAIN:	Easy town walking along streets and on part of the walls
START/PARKING:	York, Bootham Bar, GR SE602523. Car parks in York or alternatively use the Park and Ride scheme
BUS/TRAIN:	York is easily reached by train and bus from all the local towns
REFRESHMENTS:	Plenty of restaurants, wine bars, pubs and cafés in York
MAP:	*OS Explorer 290 – York*, or pick up a street map from the tourist information centre

••

This walk concentrates on taking you along some of the fascinating, narrow old streets that are found within the circuit of the city walls. It includes such diverse historic attractions as the well-preserved remains of a Roman bath house, the world-famous Jorvik Viking Centre, the medieval Merchant Adventurers' Hall, and possibly the most interesting of the four gateways in the walls. For many the highlight is a stroll along the Shambles, thronged with tourists and one of the most photographed and photogenic streets in Britain.

ⓧ ❶ **Begin by walking through Bootham Bar and along High Petergate towards the minster. Keep to the right of the church of St Mary le Belfry, continuing along High Petergate and then Low Petergate, and turn right into Grape Lane. Turn left along Swinegate and at a crossroads in front of St Sampson's church, turn right along Church Street into St Sampson's Square.**

❶ To the right, at the side of the Roman Bath pub, is the entrance to the Roman Bath Museum. These interesting remains of a Roman bath house, which lie underneath the pub, were discovered during excavations in the 1930s. Many artefacts which were found on the site are displayed in a small museum.

ⓧ **Turn left along Parliament Street and at a crossroads turn right into Coppergate. A brief detour to the left along Coppergate Walk brings you to the Jorvik Viking Centre.**

❶ The Coppergate excavations of 1979 to 1981, carried out by the York Archaeological Trust, yielded so many fascinating finds of the Viking period in York that it was decided to build a permanent centre to house and display these. It is a most imaginative museum that literally transports you back in time – you sit in backward moving trolleys – through Victorian, Georgian, Tudor, Medieval and Anglo-Saxon York to the period when Yorvik was the bustling centre of a Viking kingdom in England. During this journey you tour reconstructed streets and experience the sights, sounds and even the smells of tenth-century York. There is also a large collection of exhibits to see. Since it opened in 1984, it is not surprising that Jorvik has become one of the most popular and memorable of York's many attractions, enjoyed by visitors of all ages and nationalities.

*Walmgate Bar, the only one of York's medieval gates
to retain its Barbican*

Merchant Adventurers' Hall

⚹ **❷ Retrace your steps along Coppergate to the bottom of Parliament Street and turn right along Piccadilly.**

➀ Shortly you will pass the Merchant Adventurers' Hall on the left, an outstanding example of a medieval guildhall. It was built in the middle of the fourteenth century as a meeting place for the Merchant Adventurers, a group of merchants who invested in sometimes risky overseas trade ventures. It comprises a great hall, chapel and hospital, and is surrounded by a walled garden bordered on one side by the River Foss.

⚹ **Continue along Piccadilly and eventually the road curves right to a T-junction by Fishergate Tower. Just before reaching the T-junction an arch on the left gives you** access to a stretch of the medieval walls. Climb steps and walk along the wall, bending left to Fishergate Bar. Here you descend from the walls to cross the road, climb back onto them and continue to Walmgate Bar where you descend to street level again.

❶ Walmgate Bar was the eastern entrance into the medieval city and is of particular interest as the only one of the four gates – or bars – in York to retain its barbican, an additional defence projecting from the main gateway. The original inner gate was built in the twelfth century and the barbican was added two centuries later. It is also the only gate that has retained its portcullis.

(🚶) **❸ Turn left along Walmgate, passing St Denys' church on the left, and after crossing a bridge over the River Foss, the road continues as Fossgate. At a crossroads turn left in front of a chapel and almost immediately turn right into the Shambles.**

❶ Many would say that the Shambles is the finest and most picturesque street in Britain and at times you almost have to fight your way along it, so popular is it with visitors. The street is mentioned in Domesday Book and the name means 'street of the butchers'. People are particularly fascinated by the upper stories, some of which overhang so much that they almost meet. Look out for numbers 35 and 36, the home of the sixteenth century Catholic martyr Margaret Clitherow. She was executed for allegedly sheltering Catholic priests and holding Catholic services, a major crime in Elizabethan England.

Also look out for the first street on the right after entering the Shambles. This is Whip-Ma-Whop-Ma-Gate, the shortest street with the longest name in York! It gets its strange name because this is where petty criminals were publicly flogged.

Ⓧ At the end of the Shambles turn right through Kings Square, bear left along Low Petergate and turn right into Goodramgate.

ⓘ A gateway on the left leads into the small and secluded churchyard of Holy Trinity church. This delightful fifteenth-century building, complete with uneven floors and leaning pillars, is one York's many hidden gems.

Ⓧ ❹ Turn left in front of the National Trust shop, pass in front of St William's College, keep along the south side of the minster and follow the road back to Bootham Bar.

*Above and opposite: the Shambles, one of the most
photographed streets in Britain*

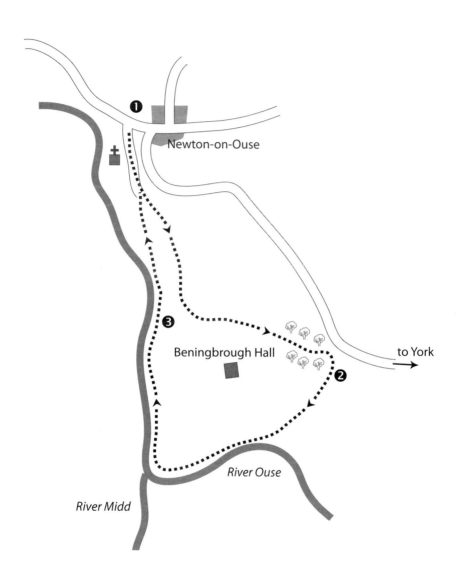

❶

Newton-on-Ouse

❸

Beningbrough Hall

to York

❷

River Ouse

River Midd

WALK 5

Beningbrough Park & the River Ouse

....

LENGTH:	8 km (5 miles)
TIME:	2.5 hours
TERRAIN:	Flat walking along a tarmac drive and tree-lined riverside paths
START/PARKING:	Newton-on-Ouse, north west of York signposted from the A19, park around the triangular village green near the church, GR SE511601
BUS/TRAIN:	Buses from York
REFRESHMENTS:	Pubs at Newton-on-Ouse, restaurant at Beningbrough Hall
MAP:	*OS Explorer 290 – York*
FROM YORK:	10 miles

....

This is an ideal walk for a languid summer afternoon. Approximately the first third of it is along a tarmac drive across the parkland surrounding Beningbrough Hall. The rest of the route is along a delightful tree-lined riverside path that follows the Ouse around a sharp bend, passing its confluence with the Nidd. From this path, there are superb views to the right across the park to the eighteenth-century hall, and to the left over the gentle and tranquil countryside of the Vale of York.

Victorian church at Newton-on-Ouse

ⓘ The pleasant village of Newton-on-Ouse is dominated by its handsome Victorian church. Although on an ancient site, the church was rebuilt in 1849 and is particularly noted for its elegant 150-foot-high tower and spire, a conspicuous landmark amidst the flat landscape of the Vale of York.

ⓧ ❶ Begin by walking along the road, signposted to Beningbrough Hall, passing to the left of the church, to reach the gateway to the park. Go through the gate and take the tarmac drive across the parkland, soon enjoying fine views of the hall.

ⓘ The grand Baroque mansion of Beningbrough Hall was built in 1716 by John Bourchier on the site of an earlier Elizabethan manor house. Its architect is thought to have been Thomas Archer, whose best-known works include Birmingham Cathedral and St John's Church in Smith Square, Westminster. As a result of its partnership with the National Portrait Gallery, Beningbrough is particularly noted for its collection of fine portraits, many of them dating back to the eighteenth century. After being in the possession of the Bourchiers for around 100 years, the estate later passed first to the Dawnays and later to the Countess of Chesterfield, and shortly after her death in 1957 it came into the ownership of the National Trust. Among its other attractions are a walled garden and the extensive parkland bordering the River Ouse.

 **Shortly after a left bend, you bear right to a fork. Continue along the left-hand drive to emerge, via a gate, onto a road. ❷ Immediately turn right along a track, at a public footpath sign. Where the track ends, walk along a narrow, enclosed footpath to the right of metal gates, by woodland on the right. Eventually the path curves right**

Beningbrough Park

to a kissing gate. Go through to re-enter the National Trust's Beningbrough Hall estate, continue along the path, go through another kissing gate and keep ahead to join the tree-lined banks of the River Ouse. After 800 m (0.5 miles), the path follows the river around a sharp right bend and opposite is where the Ouse is joined by the Nidd. Continue by the river and later the spire of Newton-on-Ouse church comes into sight. Climb a stile and keep ahead to emerge from the trees. ❸ At this point the riverside path bears slightly left but you continue straight ahead across the meadow by a line of trees on the right towards the church spire. Go through a kissing gate in the top right-hand corner of the meadow onto a track and keep ahead to a road. Bear left, here picking up the outward route, to return to the start.

Tree-lined banks of the River Ouse near Newton

The façade of Beningbrough Hall

Confluence of the rivers Ouse and Nidd

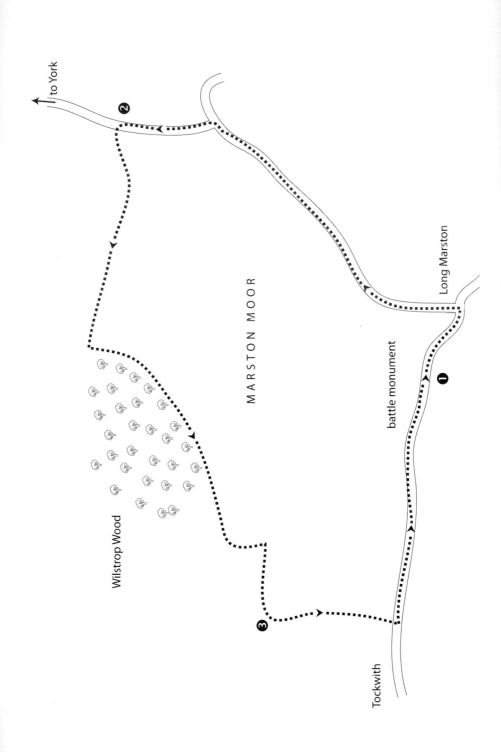

to York

❷

Long Marston

MARSTON MOOR

battle monument

❶

Wilstrop Wood

❸

Tockwith

WALK 6

Battlefield of Marston Moor

....

LENGTH:	10.5 km (6.5 miles)
TIME:	3 hours
TERRAIN:	Flat walking along lanes, tracks and field paths
START/PARKING:	Parking for a small number of cars in the layby by the battle monument on the lane between Long Marston and Tockwith, both villages are signposted from the A59 to the west of York, GR SE491521
BUS/TRAIN:	Buses from York and Wetherby
REFRESHMENTS:	None en route but pubs nearby in Long Marston and Tockwith
MAP:	OS Explorers 290 – York and 289 – Leeds
FROM YORK:	7 miles

....

The Battle of Marston Moor, fought on 2 July 1644, was one of the most important conflicts of the English Civil War. At the start of the walk there is a monument erected by the Cromwell Association in 1936 and beside it an information board. The route encircles the site of the battle, which is still open country that has never been built on, and the walking is easy, apart from the possibility of some muddy stretches after rain. There is a succession of extensive views across the flat landscape of the Vale of York.

Overlooking the battlefield of Marston Moor

ⓘ The Civil War between Charles I and Parliament broke
out in the late summer of 1642 and for the first two years
neither side had gained a decisive advantage. One of the
main reasons for this is that both sides were fairly evenly
matched, but Parliament's alliance with the Scots in 1643
helped to tilt the balance in their favour. Marston Moor
was the first major battle in which the Parliamentary army
was helped by its new Scottish allies.

The battle arose because Prince Rupert, the king's
nephew and leader of the Royalist cavalry, marched
on York to relieve the Parliamentary siege of that city.
Parliamentary forces abandoned the siege and marched
westwards to confront him. Rupert outwitted them and
entered the city from the north. He then marched out again

to do battle with the enemy and the two sides met on this flat, open and windswept area about 9.7 km (6 miles) to the west of the city. The Royalists were led by the Marquis of Newcastle and Prince Rupert, and the combined Parliamentary and Scottish army by Lord Fairfax and Lord Manchester, with Oliver Cromwell leading the cavalry.

The conflict took place during the evening. After spending most of the day deploying their troops and carrying out preliminary manoeuvres, the battle commenced around 7 pm when Cromwell's cavalry, followed by the Parliamentarian infantry, advanced on the enemy. Cromwell's cavalry charge was successful and he sent Rupert's cavalry back towards Wilstrop Wood. The Parliamentary infantry were also successful on the left wing but the right wing, led by Fairfax, suffered heavy losses against Goring and Newcastle. The turning point was when, following their initial successful charge, Cromwell's well-disciplined cavalry troops regrouped in Wilstrop Wood and swung round to attack the Royalists from behind. The Royalist army was taken completely by surprise and scattered. The result was an overwhelming victory for the Parliamentary army which only had about 300 losses, while the defeated Royalists may have lost as many as 4000. In the long term it meant that the king had virtually lost control of the north of England.

(🚶) ❶ Facing the monument, turn right along the lane towards Long Marston and on the edge of the village turn left along Atterwith Lane. After 2 km (1.25 miles) turn left along another lane, signposted to Moor Monkton and York.

(🚶) ❷ After another 800 m (0.5 miles) – where the lane bends right – turn left along a track, at a public footpath sign to Tockwith. Where the track bends right towards a

farm by a waymarked post, turn left along the right field
edge, above a ditch on the right, and the path curves right
and left to continue along the left edge of Wilstrop Wood.

❶ Wilstrop Wood was where Cromwell's cavalry troops
checked their charge and regrouped. after defeating
their Royalist counterparts They were then able to wheel
round and attack the enemy from behind, a major turning
point in the battle and one of the main reasons for the
overwhelming Parliamentary victory.

At a waymarked post by the end of a hedgeline where
the edge of the wood curves to the right, turn left along
the left field edge, and at the next post just ahead turn
right and continue in a straight line across fields following
an old hedgeline. A series of widely spaced trees mark
the way. Turn left at a hedge corner, still by a hedgeline
on the left, and at the far end of the field, turn right to
continue along the left field edge above a ditch.

❸ On emerging onto a track, turn left along it to a lane.
Turn left and follow the lane for 1.6 km (1 mile) back to
the battle monument.

Opposite: approaching Wilstrop Wood
Below: the edge of Wilstrop Wood

BATTLEFIELD OF MARSTON MOOR   41

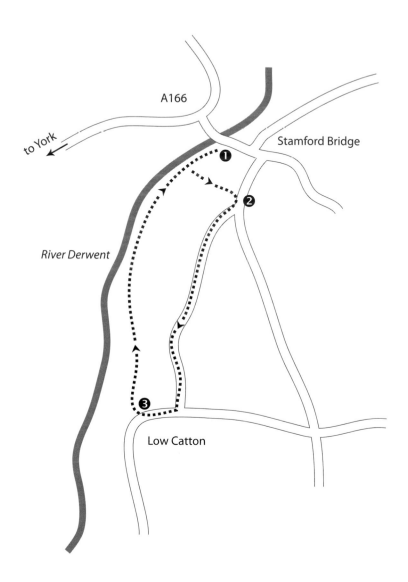

WALK 7

Stamford Bridge & Low Catton

....

LENGTH:	5.6 km (3.5 miles)
TIME:	2 hours
TERRAIN:	Flat walking mainly along lanes and riverside paths
START/PARKING:	Stamford Bridge, on the A166 to the east of York, GR SE712555. Car park and picnic area on the south side of the bridge
BUS/TRAIN:	Buses from York
REFRESHMENTS:	Pubs at Stamford Bridge, pub at Low Catton
MAP:	OS Explorer 294 – Market Weighton & Yorkshire Wolds Central
FROM YORK:	6 miles

....

From the site of a famous battle in 1066, a short stretch of riverside walking is followed by a gentle climb beside a disused viaduct onto a former railway track. Quiet lanes bring you into the hamlet of Low Catton and the final leg of the walk is an attractive stroll across meadows close to or beside the River Derwent.

❶ Everyone knows that 1066 was one of the most momentous years in English history, and the event that stands out in

River Derwent between Low Catton and Stamford Bridge

that year is the Battle of Hastings. But equally eventful was the lesser-known Battle of Stamford Bridge, which took place 20 days before the fateful encounter at Hastings and which had a most decisive impact on that later battle.

In September 1066, the English king Harold was waiting with his army on the south coast for the expected invasion by William Duke of Normandy, who claimed that he was the rightful king of England. But there was another claimant for the English throne: the Norwegian king Harald Hardrada, and in alliance with Tostig, the exiled brother of Harold, he landed on the Yorkshire coast and marched on York. After defeating a local force at Fulford just outside York on 20 September, Hardrada and Tostig received the surrender of the city. Meanwhile Harold quickly marched north to deal with this threat, covering a distance of nearly 200 miles in just five days, and arrived in York on the morning of 25 September. Hardrada and Tostig and most

of the Norwegian army were at Stamford Bridge about
6 miles away awaiting an exchange of hostages. Despite
his army being exhausted after such a long march, Harold
immediately moved to Stamford Bridge and attacked the
Norwegians, taking them by surprise.

The initial English assault was on the narrow wooden
bridge over the Derwent, a short distance upstream from
the present stone bridge. A colourful story recorded in the
Anglo-Saxon Chronicle relates that the bridge was defended
by a single giant Norwegian warrior, who could not be
dislodged until an English soldier managed to sail under
the bridge in a small boat and kill him by thrusting a long
spear up through one of the slats in the bridge.

The main battle that followed was a long, ferocious and
bloody affair but ultimately resulted in an overwhelming
victory for Harold. During the fighting both Hardrada
and Tostig were killed and this finally ended Norwegian
resistance. The precise site of the battle is uncertain but
is generally thought to be the area known as Battle Flats
on the east side of the village. Some of the battlefield has
been encroached upon by a modern housing estate but
most of it is still agricultural land. Though inaccessible, it
can be viewed from the road.

Three days after the battle, William of Normandy landed
on an undefended south coast. Harold's exhausted and
depleted army had to march back south and, as they say,
the rest is history.

**❶ From the car park and picnic area, walk back towards
the road, but before reaching it turn left, at a public
footpath sign to Low Catton, along a path which rises
gently onto a low embankment above the River Derwent.
The path bears right and descends to a kissing gate. Go
through and walk beside the river towards a disused
railway viaduct. At the viaduct, turn left along a path
beside it which heads gently up the wooded embankment.**

Turn right up steps to emerge at the top and turn left along a tarmac track, passing between the platforms of the former station, to a road.

❶ The impressive brick and cast iron viaduct carried the York to Beverley railway line across the River Derwent. Construction of the line began in 1847, was completed in 1865 and closed down exactly a century later. In the 1990s the viaduct was threatened with demolition but fortunately was saved and repaired and now forms part of a cycle network.

❷ Turn right and almost immediately right again along Low Catton Road. Continue along this lane for 1.6 km (1 mile) to a T-junction and turn right into the quiet hamlet of Low Catton.

❸ At a small triangular green turn left if visiting the pub (Gold Cup), otherwise keep to the right of the green and turn right through a kissing gate, at a public footpath sign to Stamford Bridge.

❶ It may come as something of a surprise that the off-the-beaten-track hamlet of Low Catton has a fine medieval church. It can be seen to the left of the path and occupies an attractive location close to the River Derwent. Most of it was built between 1150 and 1250 and it was restored in the Victorian era.

Walk along an enclosed path, go through a kissing gate and continue through trees to another kissing gate. Go through, keep ahead along the path and, after an enclosed stretch, the route continues along left field edges. Cross a footbridge and walk along a tree- and hedge-lined path which bends right and then curves left to a kissing gate. Go through, keep ahead through another and the path

Disused railway viaduct over the River Derwent

continues beside the river to the former railway viaduct. After passing under an arch, you rejoin the outward route and retrace your steps to the start.

The bridge over the River Derwent at Stamford Bridge

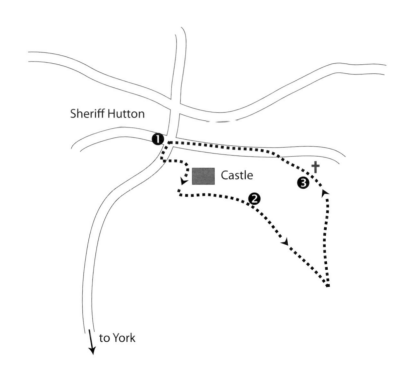

Sheriff Hutton

Castle

to York

WALK 8

Sheriff Hutton: castle & church

....

LENGTH:	3.2 km (2 miles)
TIME:	1 hour
TERRAIN:	Easy walking along clear and well-signed paths, apart from one field of long grass, uneven ground and no visible path
START/PARKING:	Sheriff Hutton, signposted from A64 between York and Malton, roadside parking near the Highwayman pub and crossroads in the village centre, GR SE651664
BUS/TRAIN:	Infrequent buses from York
REFRESHMENTS:	Pubs at Sheriff Hutton
MAP:	*OS Explorer 300 – Howardian Hills & Malton*
FROM YORK:	15 miles

....

Although only a small village, there is a lot of historic interest at Sheriff Hutton. This is mainly based around the ruined castle, once owned by one of the most powerful baronial families in England, and the medieval church, the only parish church in the country to contain the tomb of a Prince of Wales. In addition the village is surrounded by the pleasant, rolling countryside that lies between the Howardian Hills and the Vale of York.

Above and opposite: the remains of Sheriff Hutton Castle

🚶 ❶ **Begin by walking along Finkle Street (with the Highwayman on your right) and turn left along an enclosed path, at Centenary Way and Ebor Way signs. Go through a kissing gate, keep ahead towards the castle ruins and turn right through another kissing gate to continue along a fence-lined path below the castle.**

ℹ More of a fortified manor house than a castle, Sheriff Hutton was built in the late fourteenth century by John Neville, one of the leading barons in the north of England. In the following century the castle came into the possession of the powerful Richard Neville, Earl of Warwick. He was known as Warwick the Kingmaker because during the

A view of the remains of Sheriff Hutton castle

Wars of the Roses his change of allegiance from Yorkist to
Lancastrian influenced who occupied the throne. After his
death at the Battle of Barnet in 1471, the castle passed to
Richard Duke of Gloucester, brother of Edward IV, who
married Anne Neville, Warwick's daughter, the following
year. In 1483, after allegedly imprisoning his two nephews
in the Tower of London – the boy king Edward V and
his brother Richard Duke of York – Richard of Gloucester
seized the throne and became Richard III, but only had
a brief reign before his defeat and death at the Battle
of Bosworth in 1485. The castle subsequently declined
in importance and fell into ruin. Nowadays the rather
gaunt-looking ruins comprise little more than parts of the
four corner towers and a few stretches of outer wall.

ⓧ The path bends left to a kissing gate. Go through, keep ahead along a beautiful tree-lined path and go through two more kissing gates.

ⓧ ❷ After the second one, turn right and where the wire fence on the left bears left, follow a worn path beside it along the left field edge to another kissing gate in the corner. The next field is the one that is uneven and has no visible path but after going through the kissing gate, maintain the same direction across the field, heading down to the far right-hand corner where there is a gate and squeezer stile. Do not go over the stile but turn sharp left and head uphill across the field, keeping to the left of a pond and making for two trees on the low brow. Once over the brow the top of Sheriff Hutton church

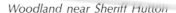

Woodland near Sheriff Hutton

tower can be seen ahead and you look out for, and head
across to, a waymarked kissing gate on the far side.
Go through, walk along the left edge of the next field
and follow the path as it veers slightly left to continue
through trees to a kissing gate which admits you to the
churchyard.

ℹ The attractive medieval church was founded by the
Normans but mainly rebuilt and enlarged in the fifteenth
century by the Nevilles. Because of the Neville connection,
it is particularly noted as being the burial place of Edward,

Above and opposite: Sheriff Hutton church, burial place of a Prince of Wales

Prince of Wales (son of Richard III and Anne Neville) who died at Sheriff Hutton in 1484 at the age of 11. It is claimed that he is the only Prince of Wales to be buried in a parish church outside London and there is a memorial to him in the church.

❸ Walk across the churchyard, keeping to the left of the church, and go through another kissing gate on the far side onto a track. Keep along the track to a road and follow it through the village back to the start.

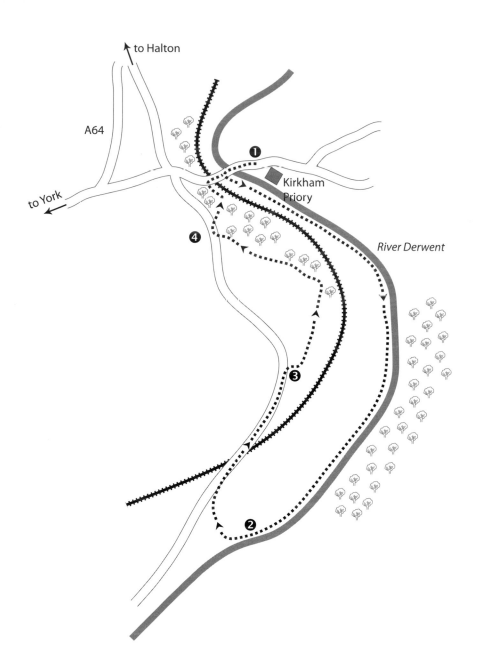

to Halton

A64

to York

①

Kirkham
Priory

River Derwent

④

③

②

WALK 9

Kirkham Priory & the Derwent Valley

....

LENGTH:	8 km (5 miles)
TIME:	2.5 hours
TERRAIN:	Undulating riverside path followed by field and woodland walking; one fairly steep descent
START/PARKING:	Kirkham Priory, signposted from the A64 between York and Malton, car park in front of the gatehouse, GR SE735658
BUS/TRAIN:	None
REFRESHMENTS:	None en route but there is a pub (Stone Trough) about 400 m (0.25 miles) to the east of the starting point
MAP:	OS Explorer 300 – Howardian Hills & Malton
FROM YORK:	16 miles

....

The walk starts with a lovely 3.6 km (2.25 mile) stretch across meadows by the tree-lined banks of the River Derwent. After leaving the river you climb gently across fields and through woodland, from where you enjoy grand views over the surrounding countryside. A final descent through woodland brings you back to the start and gives you the opportunity to explore the ruins of the medieval priory.

Above and below: River Derwent near Kirkham Priory

Gatehouse of Kirkham Priory

ⓘ You come to Kirkham Priory mainly for the gatehouse and its superb location above the River Derwent, as well as the fact that it makes a good starting point for a particularly attractive walk. There are only a few walls remaining of the church and monastic buildings but the elaborate thirteenth-century gatehouse is one of the best of its kind. The Augustinian priory was founded in the 1120s and, like all the other monastic houses in England, was closed down by Henry VIII and Thomas Cromwell in the 1530s.

🚶 ❶ Start by turning left along the road, cross Kirkham Bridge and at a public footpath sign to Howsham Bridge, turn left through a kissing gate onto a riverside path. For the next 3.6 km (2.25 miles) you keep beside the River Derwent, walking across meadows and through areas of

woodland and crossing a succession of footbridges. At one point look out for where you briefly turn right away from the river, soon turning left along a low ridge and descending to rejoin the bank. Soon after going through a gate and continuing by a wire fence on the right, you reach a waymarked gate to the right of the path.

❷ Go through it to leave the river and walk across a field, negotiating a boggy area, to a footbridge and beyond that a gate. After going through the gate, continue across two more fields to emerge onto a lane. Turn right along this narrow lane for 1.2 km (0.75 miles), crossing the railway line by Howsham signal box.

❸ Where the lane bends left, turn right over a stile and walk along a gently ascending track. Climb a stile, keep ahead and where the track bends right to a farm, continue more steeply uphill along a grassy path. At the top of the rise, keep by a fence on the left towards woodland and turn right in the field corner along the right edge of the trees. In the next corner, turn left through a gate and follow a path through the wood. Continue along the curving left inside edge of the trees to a stile, climb it and walk along a right field edge. From this height the views are particularly attractive and extensive. Veer slightly left away from the edge of the wood on the right, descend along the main track to emerge onto a road via a gate and turn right.

❹ At a public footpath sign, turn right again onto a narrow enclosed path and descend steeply through woodland. Go through a gate onto a road, turn right and follow the road over a level crossing and across Kirkham Bridge to return to the start.

Above and below: Kirkham Bridge

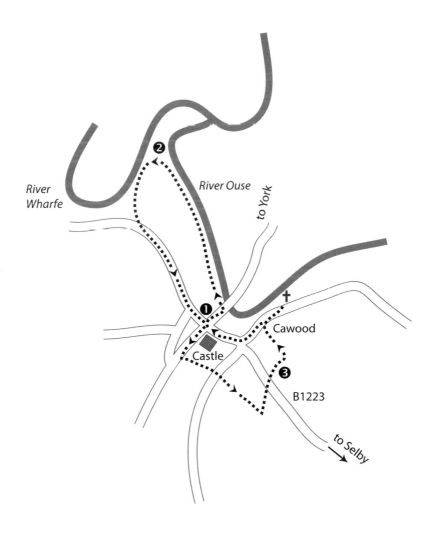

River
Wharfe

River Ouse

to York

❷

❶

Castle

Cawood

❸

B1223

to Selby

WALK 10

Cawood & the two rivers

....

LENGTH:	4.8 km (3.5 miles) or a shorter walk of 3.2 km (2 miles)
TIME:	2 hours (1 hour for the shorter version)
TERRAIN:	Field and riverside paths and quiet lanes across flat countryside
START/PARKING:	Cawood, crossroads in the village centre just off the small Market Place, GR SE574377. Parking is difficult in the narrow streets of Cawood but there are some limited spaces in Old Road near the swing bridge, otherwise park carefully in side roads
BUS/TRAIN:	Buses from York and Selby
REFRESHMENTS:	Pubs at Cawood
MAP:	OS Explorer 290 – York
FROM YORK:	10 miles

....

The two rivers are the Ouse and the Wharfe, which meet just to the north of the sleepy village of Cawood. From the village centre the walk takes you first along the banks of the Ouse and then cuts across a narrow field for a brief stroll by the Wharfe before returning to the start. This is followed by a short circuit around Cawood, passing the medieval church. The shorter version of the walk omits this circuit but unless exhausted – unlikely in view of the distance and gentle terrain – or short of time, the extra 2.4 km (1.5 miles) are well worth the effort.

Cawood Castle, former palace of the archbishops of York

ⓘ Near the village centre are the remains of Cawood Castle. The gatehouse and adjoining banqueting hall, built during the fourteenth and fifteenth centuries, are all that is left of a magnificent palace that belonged to the archbishops of York and was frequently visited by kings and church dignitaries during the Middle Ages. One of its most famous owners was Cardinal Wolsey, Henry VIII's powerful chancellor who, among his many roles and posts, was archbishop of York. After failing to get Henry a divorce from his first wife, Catherine of Aragon, Wolsey fell out of favour and it was while at Cawood in November 1530 that he was arrested for high treason. On his way to London to face almost certain execution, he fell ill and died at Leicester Abbey a few weeks later. The castle was mostly demolished in the seventeenth century but the surrounding area, Castle Garth, was later bought by the local parish council and preserved as an attractive open space.

(🚶) ❶ Start by walking along High Street in the York direction towards the swing bridge and, just before reaching it, turn left along King Street. Where the road ends, keep ahead along a paved path in front of houses and look out for a public footpath sign where you turn right up steps onto an embankment. Descend steps on the other side and at a Wolsey Walk post, turn left across a meadow to join the bank of the River Ouse. Walk along an enclosed path, cross a footbridge and continue across meadows by the tree-lined river for about 1.2 km (0.75 miles) until you reach a short waymarked post at the end of a meadow.

River Ouse near Cawood

(🚶) ❷ Turn sharp left along the right edge of the meadow, turning left in the corner to continue briefly above the River Wharfe. Follow the field edge to the left again and at a gap in the trees, turn right along a track to a road. Turn left and follow the road back to the start in Cawood.

(🚶) For the second part of the walk, turn right at the crossroads along Sherburn Street and at the public footpath and Wolsey Way signs, turn left and cross a footbridge over Bishop Dyke. Keep along the right edge of Castle Garth and go through a gate onto a lane. Turn left and almost immediately turn right, at a public footpath sign, over a stile and walk along a paved enclosed path to a gate. Go through, continue along the left edge of a playing field, cross a drive, keep ahead and in the corner

Cawood church

The Ferry Inn at Cawood

of the field, turn sharp left along an enclosed path. The path bends right to emerge onto a road. Keep ahead, curving left to a T-junction, and turn right.

❸ At the next T-junction, cross the road and continue along a track in front of a house to a gate. Go through, keep ahead along a straight path and at a T-junction, turn left along a track to a lane.

A short distance to the right is Cawood's medieval church, in a fine location on the south bank of the River Ouse. It is a predominantly Norman building, dating back to the twelfth century, but the tower was built in the fifteenth century.

Turn left along the lane to a road at a bend and turn right to return to the start, passing to the right of the castle.

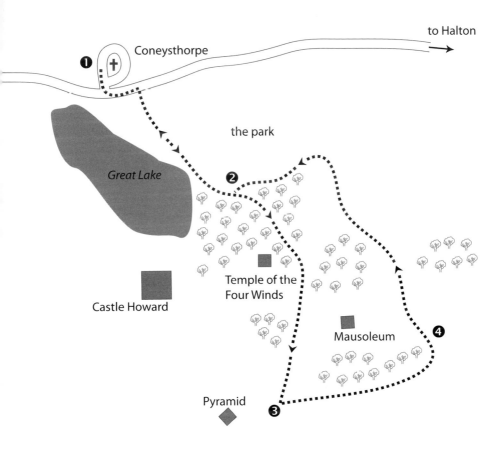

to Halton

Coneysthorpe

❶

the park

Great Lake

❷

Temple of the
Four Winds

Castle Howard

Mausoleum

❹

Pyramid

❸

WALK 11

The park at Castle Howard

LENGTH:	8.9 km (5.5 miles)
TIME:	3 hours
TERRAIN:	Mostly clear and easy tracks across landscaped parkland
START/PARKING:	Coneysthorpe, signposted from A64 between York and Malton, park around the large green near the village hall, GR SE713714
BUS/TRAIN:	None
REFRESHMENTS:	Restaurants at Castle Howard
MAP:	OS Explorer 300 – Howardian Hills & Malton
FROM YORK:	18 miles

This walk does a circuit of part of the glorious parkland surrounding Castle Howard and there are several distant views of the great house. Scattered throughout the park are a number of striking monuments and follies, and the route also passes close to some of these, creating a most interesting and absorbing walk through a largely unchanged eighteenth-century landscape.

❶ The cottages of the attractive estate village of Coneysthorpe are grouped around a large green. Near the top end is the simple and dignified Georgian chapel, built in the early nineteenth century and recently restored.

(🚶) ❶ Walk back to the road – Castle Howard can be seen on the horizon ahead – and turn left. At public footpath signs to Bog Hall and Welburn, turn right and then right again on reaching the track just ahead. Keep along it across the parkland and just after reaching the corner of woodland on the right, bear left off the track and continue along a grassy path across the corner of a field towards trees.

(🚶) ❷ On meeting a track at a fingerpost on the edge of the woodland, keep ahead through the trees along a narrow path, in the Welburn direction, and at a track turn right to a kissing gate. Go through, keep ahead and where the wall on the right bears right, keep straight ahead across the grass to a fence corner and fingerpost. Bear right and head uphill over the brow of a hill, between woodland on the left and the Temple of the Four Winds on the right. At the brow, head down to the New River Bridge, go through a kissing gate and cross the bridge. Pause and look to the right in order to enjoy the finest view on the walk of the great house.

The small, early nineteenth-century chapel at Coneysthorpe

Temple of the Four Winds

The Pyramid, one of the many monuments and follies in the park

ⓘ By any standards Castle Howard, home of the Howard
family for over 300 years, ranks as one of the grandest
of the great country houses of England. It was designed
for Charles Howard, third Earl of Carlisle, by Sir John
Vanbrugh, one of the foremost architects of the day,
assisted by Nicholas Hawksmoor, another renowned
architect. Although it took over 100 years to complete,
most of it was built between 1699 and 1712. It is an
outstanding example of the Baroque style and is particularly
noted for the great dome, an particular feature of English
country houses. Inside, the opulent state rooms contain
a vast collection of paintings, china, furniture and statues
that have been acquired by the Howards over the
centuries. Some of these treasures were destroyed by a
great fire in November 1940 which caused widespread
devastation to the house, severely damaging the dome and
around 20 rooms. Soon after the end of World War II a
comprehensive programme of restoration began, but such
was the scale of the damage, this was not fully completed
until the mid 1990s.

ⓘ Surrounding the great house are the formal gardens and
beyond them around 1000 acres of landscaped parkland
that includes lakes, fountains and a variety of structures,
all erected during the first half of the eighteenth century.
Many of these can be seen on the walk. The Temple of
the Four Winds, built between 1723 and 1738, has already
been passed. A little further on in the distance you see the
Pyramid, designed by Hawksmoor in 1728, and later on
come fine views of the Mausoleum, constructed between
1728 and 1736 and the burial place of the Howards.

**ⓚ From the bridge keep ahead along a straight track to a
fingerpost. ❸ Turn left along a tarmac track, following
the sign for Huttons Ambo. At the next fingerpost turn
left, in the Coneysthorpe direction, and turn left again at**

the next footpath sign by farm buildings. After crossing
a footbridge over a brook, the track bends left and
continues to a farm (Bog Hall).

❹ Follow the track through the farm buildings and
around a left bend – there is a footpath sign to
Coneysthorpe half-hidden in the trees here. At the next
fingerpost ❷, turn right off the track onto a grassy path,
here picking up the outward route, and retrace your steps
to the start.

Distant view of Castle Howard

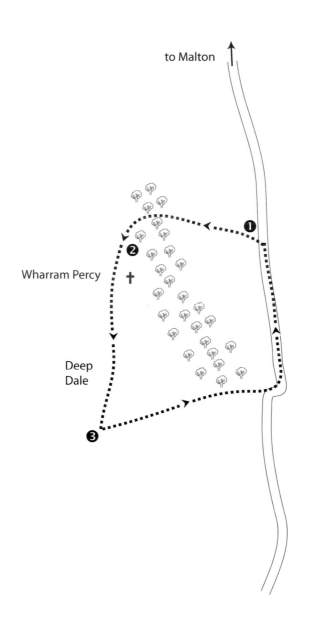

to Malton

❶

❷

Wharram Percy

✝

Deep
Dale

❸

WALK 12

Wharram Percy: a deserted medieval village

....

LENGTH:	4.8 km (3 miles)
TIME:	1.5 hours
TERRAIN:	One modest descent and ascent, otherwise fairly flat and easy walking on well-signed paths, track and a lane
START/PARKING:	Wharram Percy, follow signs from B1248 about 7 miles south of Malton, GR SE866645
BUS/TRAIN:	None
REFRESHMENTS:	None
MAP:	OS Explorer 300 – Howardian Hills & Malton
FROM YORK:	24 miles

....

A short descent into a valley brings you to the fascinating and atmospheric remains of the deserted medieval village of Wharram Percy. After a walk through the village and a visit to the church, you climb above the steep-sided valley of Deep Dale and keep along the edge of it, enjoying magnificent views over the rolling countryside of the Yorkshire Wolds. The remainder of the walk is a flat and easy stroll along a field path and a quiet lane.

Descending towards Wharram Percy

(symbol) ❶ **Start by taking the path, signposted to 'Wharram Percy, Deserted Medieval Village', that leads off from the car park downhill to a kissing gate. Go through, continue more steeply downhill, go through a kissing gate, bear slightly right and go through another kissing gate. Descend steps, cross a footbridge, go up a short flight of steps and after going through a kissing gate, walk along a track, heading uphill through the middle of the deserted village.**

❶ There are around 3000 sites of deserted villages scattered throughout England but Wharram Percy is the finest and most extensively excavated, researched and investigated example. The investigation began in the early 1950s and lasted for over 40 years. This village, tucked away in a fold of the Yorkshire Wolds, has had a long period of occupation and was at its height around the beginning of the fourteenth century. It does not appear to have been too devastated by the Black Death of 1349, but became depopulated during the fifteenth century as a result of the profitability of the wool trade at the time and the spread of sheep farming. Looking after flocks of sheep requires far fewer people than growing crops and by the beginning of the sixteenth century Wharram Percy had become virtually deserted.

On the hillside above the track to the right the outlines of peasant houses and the manor house can be discerned by looking carefully at the bumps in the ground and reading the various information panels. At the far end of the village is the church, the only substantial surviving building. As you walk around the ruins, it is interesting to trace its history throughout the ages, noticing that the church building expanded and contracted in line with the fluctuations in the population of the village. Even after Wharram Percy became deserted, it continued to be used as a place of worship by people from some of the nearby villages until the late nineteenth century and only fell into its present ruinous state after the lead on its roof was stolen in 1949.

Ruined church at Wharram Percy

(🧍) ❷ At a fork take the left-hand lower track, passing to the right of a farm building, to a kissing gate. Go through, keep ahead to the church, pass in front of it and continue along a grassy path which bends left between a stream and former mill and fish pond. Head up to go through a kissing gate, bear right and continue up across a sloping field, making for a public footpath sign. Bear right and keep along the top left edge of the field above the steep-sided valley of Deep Dale.

(🧍) ❸ On reaching a footpath post at the corner of woodland, turn sharp left over a stile, signposted Centenary Way, and walk along the right edge of a field, by a bank and hedgeline on the right. Later the path keeps along the right edge of a belt of woodland to a gate. Go through onto a lane, keep ahead and follow the lane around a left bend and on back to the car park.

Steep-sided valley of Deep Dale, on the fringes of the Yorkshire Wolds

Climbing out of Wharram Percy

Foundations of the manor house

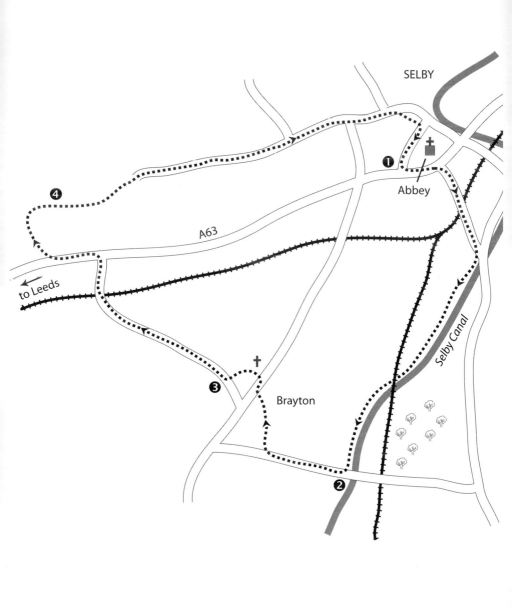

SELBY

❹

A63

to Leeds

❶

Abbey

❸

Brayton

❷

Selby Canal

WALK 13
Selby: abbey & canal

....

LENGTH:	9.7 km (6 miles)
TIME:	3 hours
TERRAIN:	Flat walking on field paths, roads and a canal towpath
START/PARKING:	Selby, Market Place, GR SE615324. Car parks at Selby
BUS/TRAIN:	Buses from York and Leeds; trains from Hull and Leeds
REFRESHMENTS:	Pubs and cafés at Selby
MAP:	OS Explorer 290 – York
FROM YORK:	14 miles

....

The first part of the route is along the towpath of the Selby Canal which quickly leads you out of the town into pleasant, open countryside. A combination of roads and paths brings you to Brayton's impressive church, from where you continue along a lane and field paths, crossing Selby Drain. Near the end of the walk, there is a fine view of Selby Abbey. All the way there are wide and extensive views across the surrounding flat terrain.

❶ The Benedictine abbey of Selby, founded in 1069 shortly after the Norman Conquest, is one of the finest churches in the country and one of a handful of monastic churches that have survived more or less intact. This is because the local people bought it for use as a parish church after the monastery was dissolved by Henry VIII in 1539.

The impressive Norman nave, built in the twelfth century, is modelled on that of Durham Cathedral. In contrast, the east end was rebuilt in the fourteenth century in the contemporary Gothic style. Throughout its history, Selby Abbey has suffered a number of disasters, including fires and subsidence. A particularly destructive fire occurred in 1906 soon after the church had been comprehensively restored by the Victorians, but three years later the damage had been repaired.

❶ The walk starts at the top end of the market place in front of the abbey. Pass to the right of the abbey, turn right along Park Street and keep ahead over the railway bridge. Where the road bends right, bear left, cross Canal Road and turn right onto the towpath of the Selby Canal.

Opposite: Selby Abbey
Below: the peaceful Selby Canal

ℹ️ The Selby Canal was built in 1776 to link the River Ouse with the Aire and Calder Navigation, a distance of just under 6 miles. It was initially busy and successful, carrying agricultural produce, coal and cloth, and there was even a flourishing passenger trade between Selby and Hull. The cutting of a new, larger canal and the advent of the railways brought about its decline and it is now chiefly used for pleasure.

🚶 **Keep by the canal for the next 1.6 km (1 mile), passing under a road bridge and railway bridge.**

(⊼) ❷ At a small car park by Brayton Bridge, turn right along a road into Brayton. After just under 800 m (0.5 miles), look out for a public footpath sign on the right where you turn onto an enclosed path, passing to the right of a bungalow. Go through a chain stile and the path becomes a tarmac one which you walk along to emerge onto a road in a new housing area. Turn right, curving first left and then right, and turn left into Engelhart Close. Where the road ends, keep ahead along a fence-lined, tarmac path and go through another chain stile. Turn right along an enclosed path and turn left to keep along a left field edge, later by garden fences on the left, to emerge onto a road. Turn right and just before reaching Brayton church, turn left along a tarmac track.

❶ The imposing tower and spire of Brayton church dominates the surrounding flat landscape for many miles. The site of the church is an ancient one and until the dissolution of the monasteries in the 1530s, it was closely linked with Selby Abbey. The present building dates mainly from the fourteenth and fifteenth centuries.

(⊼) At a public footpath sign by one of the entrances to the churchyard, turn left and walk along the right edge of a field to a lane.

(⊼) ❸ Turn right and at a fork, take the left-hand lane (Brackenhill Lane). Continue along it for just under 1.6 km (1 mile) and after a level crossing, keep ahead between houses to a T-junction. Turn left – there is a pavement on the right-hand side of the road – and after 400 m (0.25 miles) turn right, at a public footpath sign Selby Horseshoe, and walk along a raised path between fields to a stile. Climb it, keep ahead to a waymarked post and follow the direction of the yellow arrow to the left across the field (this section may be muddy) to a footbridge over

Selby Drain. Cross it, continue along the right field edge and in front of a gate, turn left over a stile. Walk along an enclosed path which bends right to another stile.

❹ After climbing it, turn right along another enclosed path which emerges onto a drive. Continue along it, passing to the left of farm buildings and gradually curving right. The drive becomes a lane which you follow to a T-junction on the edge of Selby. Turn right along a road and after 1.6 km (1 mile), look out for a public footpath sign where you turn right into Dam Bank. At the end of the road, turn left in front of a house onto a path which bends right and emerges into a grassy area. Keep along its left edge and bear left alongside Selby Drain to a road. Turn right, cross a bridge over the drain and turn right again to return to the market place.

Tower and spire of Brayton church

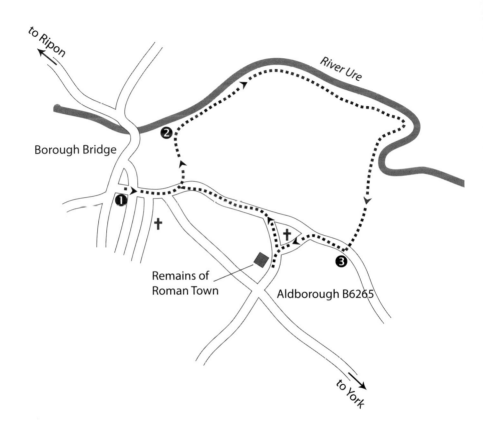

to Ripon

River Ure

Borough Bridge

2

1

✝

Remains of
Roman Town

✝

3

Aldborough B6265

to York

WALK 14

Boroughbridge & Aldborough

. . . .

LENGTH:	6.4 km (4 miles)
TIME:	2 hours
TERRAIN:	Flat walking along roads, lanes and field and riverside paths
START/PARKING:	Boroughbridge, St James Square, GR SE396666. Car park at Boroughbridge
BUS/TRAIN:	Buses from York and Ripon
REFRESHMENTS:	Pubs and cafés at Boroughbridge, pub at Aldborough
MAP:	OS Explorer 299 – Ripon & Boroughbridge
FROM YORK:	20 miles

. . . .

A large proportion of this pleasant and relaxing stroll
is beside the River Ure and there are fine and largely
unimpeded views across the wide expanses of the Vale of
York. About two thirds of the way round you pass through
the quiet village of Aldborough, site of a Roman town, with
a maypole and stocks on the village green and a monument
to a fourteenth-century battle. The route is easy to follow
as it is well-waymarked throughout with white arrows on a
purple background.

River Ure between Boroughbridge and Aldborough

ⓘ The Normans created the first settlement at Boroughbridge
in the late eleventh century. A wooden bridge was built
over the River Ure, subsequently rebuilt in stone and
regularly upgraded and widened over the centuries. This
river crossing made the town an important point on the
Great North Road, especially during the heyday of stage
coach travel in the eighteenth century. The church was
built on its present site in 1851 and the elaborate fountain
in St James Square, where the walk starts, was built over
a well in 1875. On the western side of the town stand the
Devil's Arrows, three prehistoric standing stones.

**Ⓧ ❶ From the fountain in St James Square walk along
Aldborough Road. Where the main road bends right, keep
ahead along a lane (still in the Aldborough direction)
and at a public footpath sign, turn left through a kissing
gate. Walk along an enclosed path and on reaching a low
embankment above the River Ure, bear right to ascend it.**

ⓘ The fields around here on both sides of the river were part
of the site of the Battle of Boroughbridge. The battle was

fought on 16 March 1322 between the forces of Edward
II and rebel troops, led by Thomas Earl of Lancaster, who
were discontented with what they perceived as the weak
rule of the king. The key strategic places in the battle were
a nearby ford and a bridge over the river a short distance
upstream from here, not far from the present road bridge.

Elaborate fountain at the start of the walk in Boroughbridge

Sir Andrew Harclay, leader of the king's army, controlled
the bridge and the rebel forces were on the other side. It
was a short and one-sided battle. The royal army greatly
outnumbered the rebels and had an easy victory. The Earl
of Lancaster suffered the usual fate of rebel leaders and was
subsequently executed at Pontefract Castle.

❷ For the next 2 km (1.25 miles) you keep along this
embankment above the river, going through a series of
kissing gates. Eventually you follow the Ure around a
sharp right bend and soon after the next kissing gate, the
path leaves the river and emerges onto an enclosed track.
Keep along the track to a lane.

(🚶) ❸ Turn right into Aldborough, bear left along the side of a green and turn left through the village to a larger green with a maypole. Bear left and continue up to the entrance to the Roman site.

❶ The Romans built the town of *Isurium Brigantes* on the site of the tribal capital of the Brigantes in 72 AD near a ford over the River Ure. Of the Roman settlement all that remains are a few low walls, two fine mosaics and a small museum on the site. The small, quiet village of Aldborough was once the main settlement in the area but declined after the main crossing point over the river moved to Boroughbridge.

(🚶) Retrace your steps to the first green and keep to the left of it, passing to the left of the medieval church, to a road junction by the Battle Stone, which commemorates the Battle of Boroughbridge. At the junction bear left and follow the lane back to the start.

Opposite: Maypole
Below: stocks on the village green at Aldborough

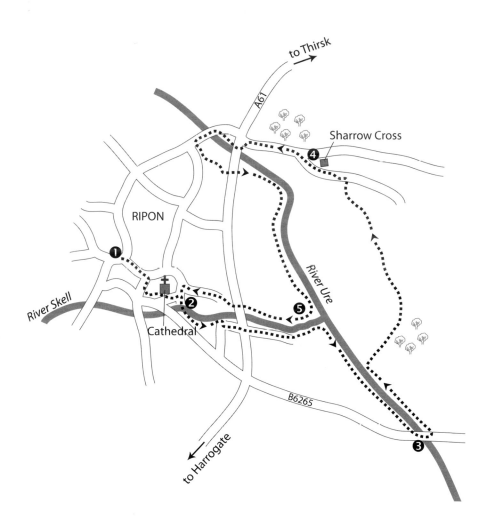

WALK 15

Ripon & Sharow

....

LENGTH:	8.9 km (5.5 miles)
TIME:	3 hours
TERRAIN:	Flat walking mainly along riverside paths
START/PARKING:	Ripon, Market Place, GR SE313713. Car parks at Ripon
BUS/TRAIN:	Buses from York and Harrogate
REFRESHMENTS:	Pubs and cafés at Ripon, pub at Sharow
MAP:	OS Explorer 299 – Ripon & Boroughbridge
FROM YORK:	31 miles

....

Apart from a stretch across fields and along roads near
Sharow, the vast bulk of this walk is on riverside paths
beside the Skell and Ure to the east of Ripon city centre.
There are fine views along both rivers, pleasant walking on
field paths and tracks when approaching Sharow, and distant
views across fields of Ripon Cathedral on the return leg. The
walk has a religious theme as, apart from the cathedral, part
of it follows the Sanctuary Way, which marks the ancient
Sanctuary Boundary around Ripon, and passes the one
remaining Sanctuary Cross at Sharow.

❶ Ripon's history as a religious centre stretches back to
Anglo-Saxon times. The first monastery was founded in
the seventh century and St Wilfrid began the building

West Front of Ripon Cathedral

of the first stone church in 672. Surprisingly, the crypt survives from the early Saxon church, the only piece of Saxon architecture to be found in an English cathedral. Throughout the Middle Ages Ripon was a collegiate church,

served by a college of canons, and – like Beverley Minster
– served as a sub-cathedral for the diocese of York. It
became a full cathedral when a new diocese of Ripon
was created in 1836. The present building, one of the
smaller English cathedrals, dates mainly from the thirteenth
and fourteenth centuries. Apart from the Saxon crypt, it is
particularly noted for the lancet windows on the plain but
beautifully proportioned west front, fine east window and
the intricate carvings on the fifteenth-century choir stalls.

**① From the market place, take the narrow street that
leads off from one corner of it (Kirkgate) to the west**

Walking beside the River Ure

front of the cathedral. Keep to the right of the cathedral and walk along the tarmac path that runs along its south side, heading downhill and curving right to emerge onto a road (High Street Agnesgate). Turn left, at a T-junction turn right, and where the road ends keep ahead and cross a footbridge over the River Skell.

(⚉) ❷ On the other side, turn left along a concrete path beside the river to a road, cross over and continue along Fisher Green (signposted Ripon Rowel Walk North). Pass under a road bridge, keep ahead and where the road ends, continue along a riverside path to the meeting of the Skell and Ure. Here the path bears right to continue beside the tree-lined banks of the larger river. Follow the path as it curves to the right, cross a footbridge over a stream and continue above the left edge of fields, later rejoining the river bank.

(⚉) ❸ At Hewick Bridge, go up steps onto a road, turn left over the bridge and at a public footpath sign to Sharow, turn left to continue the walk along the opposite bank of the Ure, here joining the Sanctuary Way.

❶ The Sanctuary Way Walk was created in 2005 by the local rotary clubs to celebrate the centenary of Rotary International. It follows the boundary of the area around Ripon within which anyone could be given sanctuary overnight, a right first granted by King Aethelstan in 937. The line of the boundary was marked by eight crosses, of which only one – shortly to be passed on the route – remains. The right of sanctuary continued until the Reformation.

(⚉) Look out for a waymarked post where the path forks and take the right-hand path away from the river to continue along the left edge of a field. Just before

Approaching the village of Sharow

reaching the edge of trees, turn left to a waymarked gate, go through, turn right and keep along the right edge of fields, by woodland on the right. As you continue along a hedge-lined path, fine views open up ahead looking across fields to the tower of Sharow's early nineteenth-century church. The path later widens into a track and eventually bends right to emerge onto a road on the edge of the village of Sharow. Turn right for the pub; otherwise the route continues to the left to reach a T-junction by Sharow Cross.

ℹ️ Sharow Cross, now in the care of the National Trust, is the only one of the eight sanctuary crosses around Ripon that has survived.

🚶 ❹ At the T-junction, turn left along Dishforth Road and where the road bears right to a traffic island, keep ahead

Sharow Cross

along a tarmac track to pass under a road bridge, here rejoining the River Ure. Keep ahead to a T-junction, turn left to cross a bridge over the river, take the first road on the left and just before it curves right, turn left along a track to a kissing gate. Go through, keep ahead to go through another and walk along a tarmac path, passing under the road bridge that you went under earlier. Continue along a riverside path, go through a kissing gate and keep ahead.

⑤ Just before reaching the confluence of the Ure and Skell, follow the path as it curves right and continue by the River Skell. Go through a kissing gate by the side of a house, keep ahead to join a tarmac track and pass under a road bridge. On emerging onto a road, keep ahead to a junction, pass to the left of a small triangular green and continue along Low Mill Road. Follow the road around a right bend, here rejoining the outward route, and take the first road on the left (High Street Agnesgate). Retrace your steps past the cathedral to return to the start.

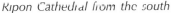

Ripon Cathedral from the south

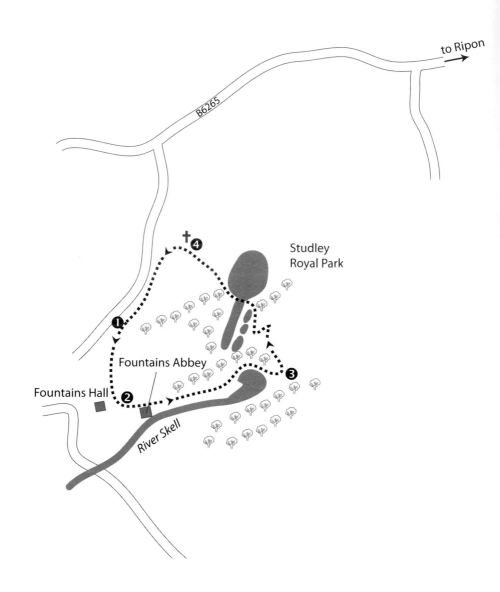

WALK 16
Fountains Abbey & Studley Royal

....

LENGTH:	4.8 km (3 miles)
TIME:	1.5 hours
TERRAIN:	Easy walking through parkland, mainly on tarmac paths
START/PARKING:	Fountains Abbey Visitor Centre, signposted from A61 between Harrogate and Ripon, GR SE273687
BUS/TRAIN:	Infrequent buses from Ripon throughout the year from Monday to Saturday, more regular buses from Ripon on Sundays and Bank Holiday Mondays from the beginning of April to the end of September
REFRESHMENTS:	Restaurant at the Visitor Centre, tea room at Lakeside entrance
MAP:	*OS Explorers 298 – Nidderdale or 299 – Ripon & Boroughbridge*
FROM YORK:	33 miles

....

This fascinating walk may be relatively short and could be completed in well under 2 hours but it is so packed with historic interest, magnificent architecture and outstanding views that you could well spend most of the day over it. It includes all the main features of the Studley Royal Estate:

Tudor hall, medieval abbey, eighteenth-century water garden and Victorian church. The estate, a World Heritage site, is owned and maintained by the National Trust and there is an admission charge, but it is worth every penny.

(🚶) ❶ From the visitor centre take the tarmac path, signposted to Abbey, Water Garden, Mill and Fountains Hall. Go through a gate, keep ahead and the path bends right and gently descends to a gate on the edge of trees. Go through and at a fork immediately ahead, take the right-hand path, signposted to Fountains Hall, which continues down through the trees and bends left to a T-junction beside the hall.

❶ The fine Elizabethan mansion of Fountains Hall was partly built with stones from the recently redundant abbey in the

Fountains Hall

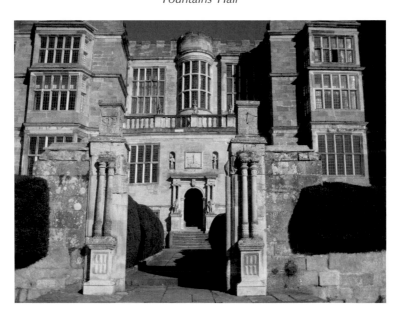

Above and below: Fountains Abbey

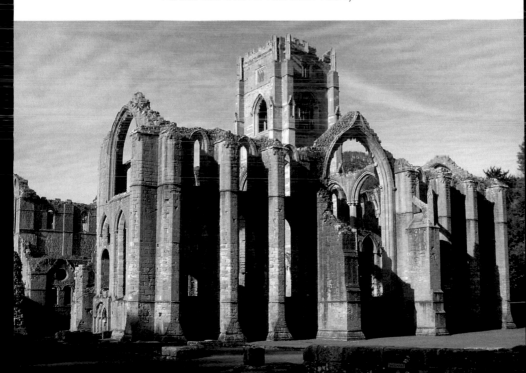

late sixteenth century. It later became redundant itself but was modernised and restored in the 1920s and 30s. It fell into disrepair after World War II but was restored again by the National Trust who acquired the estate in 1983. Although part of the hall has been converted into flats, some rooms are open to the public.

(人) **At the T-junction turn left and soon the imposing remains of Fountains Abbey come into view.**

ⓘ Fountains Abbey, probably the finest monastic ruin in Europe, is simply overwhelming. Its remains are so extensive and well-preserved that nowhere else in Britain can you get a clearer idea of what monastic life was like in the Middle Ages. The scale of the buildings clearly indicates that this was not just a religious community but the heart

Viewing the interior of Fountains Abbey

of a business empire, a vast and highly successful capitalist enterprise.

The Cistercian abbey was founded in 1132 by a group of Benedictine monks from St Mary's Abbey in York, discontented with the lax standards there. By the time it was dissolved in 1539 by Henry VIII and Thomas Cromwell, it had become one of the greatest and wealthiest monasteries in England, owning vast areas of farmland, sheep pastures, quarries, lead mines and fisheries in Yorkshire. The abbey church, which dwarfs many cathedrals, is an outstanding example of the Transitional style of the later twelfth century, combining heavy rounded Norman pillars with pointed Gothic arches. The last part of the church, the tower which rises above the north transept, was completed not long before the abbey was closed down. Adjoining the church are the extensive domestic buildings grouped round the cloisters – dormitories, refectories, infirmary, kitchens, storehouses, wash rooms and guest accommodation. These are unusually complete and merit a lengthy inspection. Particularly impressive is the great, stone-vaulted cellarium (used for storage and as a dining hall), over 300 feet long and occupying the whole of the western side of the cloisters. Also look out for the three cells underneath the abbot's house, used to imprison monks who broke the monastic rules.

(🚶) ❷ **To continue the walk, take the path to the left of the abbey church through the valley of the little River Skell to the water garden. Immediately after a left bend, turn right onto a tarmac path, cross the Rustic Bridge over a channel, and at a fork continue along the right-hand path which curves right around the side of the water. Look out for where you bear left onto an uphill path through trees, signposted Anne Boleyn's Seat, and at the top turn sharp left to reach a magnificent viewpoint over the garden.**

i The view from Anne Boleyn's Seat takes in a broad sweep of the garden which, with its formal design, pools, grand vistas, follies and the ruins of the abbey, reveals exactly what its owner and creator was trying to achieve. He was John Aislabie, an ambitious politician who acquired the Studley Royal Estate in 1699. Initially he concentrated on his political career, rising to the position of Chancellor of the Exchequer in 1718, but lost his job and was expelled from Parliament because of his involvement in the South Sea Bubble in 1720, the major financial scandal of the age. Returning to his Yorkshire estate in disgrace, he devoted the rest of his life to the creation of the water garden, based largely on contemporary French designs. After his death in 1742 his son William carried on with his grand project and it was he who put the finishing touches to the garden by purchasing the adjacent Fountains Abbey Estate and acquiring the extensive monastic ruins as the ultimate in garden ornaments. The estate later passed to the Vyner family and since 1983 has been owned and maintained by

Looking back to Fountains Abbey from Anne Boleyn's Seat

Temple of Fame

the National Trust. It acquired World Heritage Site status in 1986.

Over the next 800 m (0.5 miles) you either pass or see from a distance many of the main features of the garden. First is the Temple of Fame which, despite its stone-like appearance, was built from wood and plaster. Next comes the Octagon Tower, another fine viewpoint, and this is followed by the Serpentine Tunnel, which was built to enable carriages to descend to the lower level. At the bottom, the Temple of Piety, a perfect replica of a Classical temple, can be seen to the left.

(🚶) ❸ Keep ahead through woodland, bending first right and then left, to the Temple of Fame. Continue to the Octagon Tower, and just beyond it turn sharp left through the Serpentine Tunnel and descend through woodland to a T-junction at the bottom. Turn sharp right along the lakeside tarmac path, curving left to cross a bridge over the lake. Keep ahead to a T-junction, turn right and pass through a gate beside ornamental gates to leave the water gardens and enter the deer park. At a fork ahead, take the left-hand path up to a car park and walk across it, bearing slightly left and heading gently uphill across grass to a footpath sign to St Mary's Church and Visitor Centre. Here you pick up an obvious path and continue up to the church.

❶ St Mary's church was built by the Vyner family, owners of the estate at the time, in memory of Frederick Vyner who was murdered by Greek bandits in 1870. The family commissioned one of the foremost architects of the day, William Burges, who is perhaps best known for his work on the restoration and rebuilding of Cardiff Castle and Castell Coch in south Wales, and it is a particularly impressive example of Victorian Gothic architecture.

(🚶) ❹ At a tarmac path in front of the church, turn left, go through a gate and turn left along a tree-lined path. The path keeps parallel to a road on the right to return you to the start.

The grand Victorian church of St Mary

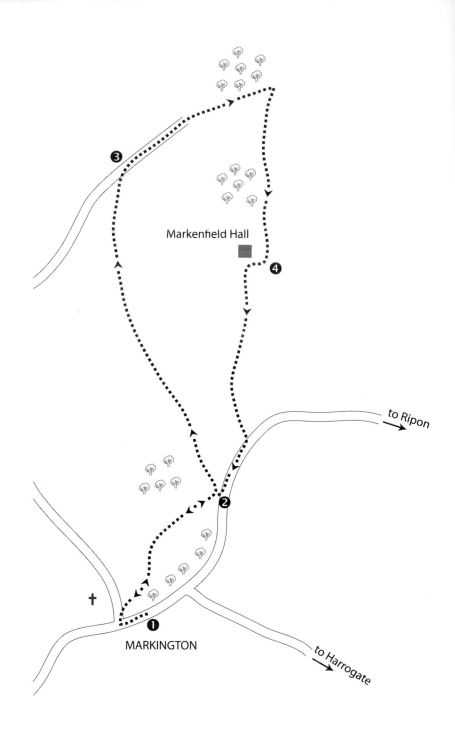

Markenfield Hall

MARKINGTON

to Ripon

to Harrogate

WALK 17

Markenfield Hall

....

LENGTH:	8.9 km (5.5 miles)
TIME:	3 hours
TERRAIN:	Tracks and field paths across gently undulating country, expect some muddy stretches after wet weather
START/PARKING:	Markington, signposted from the A61 between Harrogate and Ripon, GR SE287650. Park in the village street near the Yorkshire Hussar pub
BUS/TRAIN:	Infrequent buses from Ripon
REFRESHMENTS:	Pubs at Markington
MAP:	*OS Explorers 298 – Nidderdale* or *299 – Ripon & Boroughbridge*
FROM YORK:	28 miles

....

From the village of Markington, the route guides you
along paths and tracks, across fields and by small areas of
woodland. At several points there are fine and extensive
views across the surrounding gently undulating countryside
to the line of the Hambleton Hills, the western edge of the
North York Moors. The highlight and chief feature of historic
interest is the moated Markenfield Hall, a picturesque
medieval manor house standing in an isolated location and
approached from across fields.

Woodland near Markington

(🚶) ❶ With your back to the pub, turn left along the village street and turn right along a lane signposted to Fountains Abbey. Over to the left is the small nineteenth-century church. Just after crossing the bridge over a beck, bear right along a tarmac track and go through a kissing gate. Walk along the left edge of a sports field, bending first left and then right, and turn left up a short flight of steps behind goalposts. Continue along the left edge of the field in front, go through a kissing gate in the corner and keep ahead along a track across the next field towards a group of buildings. Go through a gate and continue along a track to a lane.

(🚶) ❷ Immediately turn left, at a public footpath sign, along an enclosed path to a stile. Climb it, keep ahead along a gently ascending, narrow, hedge-lined path and continue through an area of woodland to a stile. After climbing it, keep ahead and go through a hedge gap onto a lane. Turn right but almost immediately turn left over a stone stile, climb another stile and keep ahead across a field. On the far side near the left-hand corner, go through a gate and continue along a track, passing farm buildings on the right and curving slightly left to a gate. Go through, walk along a right field edge, climb a stile in the corner, keep ahead to cross a track, climb another stile opposite and walk through a young conifer plantation. At a T-junction, keep ahead over a stile and continue across the plantation towards a low wooded hill on the far side. Bear right along the base of that hill to a stile, climb it onto a track, immediately turn left through a gate and continue along the right edge of the next three fields, going through two gates. On this stretch of the walk there are fine views across the fields to the right to the distant outline of the Hambleton Hills. A few yards after entering the third field, look out for a blue waymark which directs you to bear right through a gap and continue across the middle of the next field. Go through a gate on the far side, head across a field, keeping close to its left edge, go through another gate and bear right over the lower slopes of a low hill to a gate. After going through it, head gently downhill along a track which curves first right and then left to skirt a marshy area and keep across a field towards farm buildings. Climb a stile into the farmyard and keep ahead between the farm buildings to emerge onto a lane.

(※) ❸ Turn right and the lane becomes an enclosed track which keeps along the right edge of conifer woodland and heads gently down into a dip and then up to reach a T-junction. Ahead are more fine views of the Hambleton Hills. Turn sharp right along a track and after going through a gate, keep ahead – leaving the track – along the right field edge to another gate. Continue along the right edge of the next two fields and in the second field the path curves gradually left along the left edge of woodland. Look out for where a public footpath sign directs you to turn right over a stone stile into the woodland, immediately turn left, turn right over a plank footbridge, climb a stile and head diagonally across a field towards Markenfield Hall. Climb a stile and keep ahead to pass in front of the hall.

❶ When viewed from across the moat, Markenfield Hall is everyone's idea of what a fortified medieval manor house should look like, and it is one of the finest and most authentic examples of its kind in the country. The mellowed stone buildings, grouped around a courtyard and entered via a gatehouse, date mainly from the early fourteenth century and were built by the Markenfield family. Over the following centuries the Markenfields achieved a high standing and level of prosperity through service to the monarchy, but unfortunately their fortunes

Above and below: Markentield Hall

came to an abrupt end in 1569. As a Catholic family, they became involved in the Rising of the North, a rebellion which aimed to remove the Protestant Elizabeth I from the throne and replace her with her cousin, the Catholic Mary Queen of Scots. The revolt failed, the Markenfields were forced to flee into exile and the house was confiscated.

After nearly two centuries of neglect, Markenfield Hall was bought by the Grantley family in 1761 who began the long process of restoration. They made it a family home again and their descendants still live in the hall today. Public admittance is limited to certain afternoons in May and June; for details phone 01765 692303.

❹ **At the end of the buildings, turn right along a tarmac drive. Turn left through a waymarked gate, keep ahead along a track across a field and continue along the left edge of the next field. Climb a stile in the corner, walk along an enclosed track and on entering the next field, head diagonally across it to a stile on the far side. After climbing it, turn left along an enclosed track to a lane. Turn right and where the lane bends left, keep ahead along a track and go through a gate.** ❷ **Here you rejoin the outward route and retrace your steps to the start.**

Winter landscape near Markington

Small nineteenth-century church at Markington

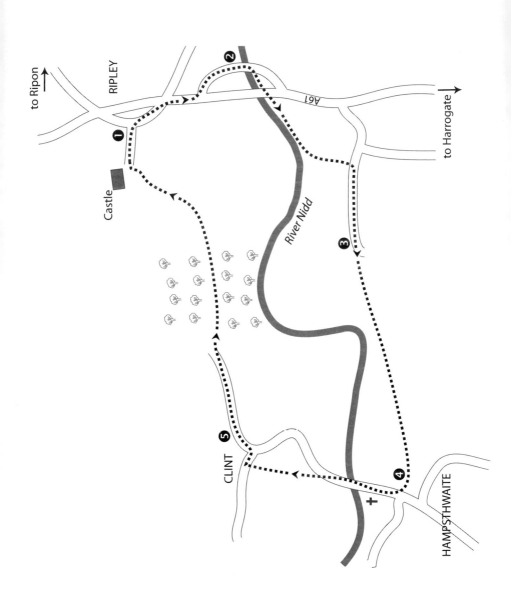

WALK 18

Ripley, Hampsthwaite & the Nidd Valley

LENGTH:	8 km (5 miles)
TIME:	2.5 hours
TERRAIN:	Well-marked riverside, field and woodland paths and tracks; some modest climbs
START/PARKING:	Ripley village centre in front of the Boars Head, GR SE285605. Car park at Ripley
BUS/TRAIN:	Buses from Harrogate and Ripon
REFRESHMENTS:	Pub and café at Ripley
MAP:	OS Explorer 298 – Nidderdale
FROM YORK:	23 miles

From the starting point above the valley of the Nidd, you twice descend to the river and climb back out of the valley. There is much pleasant walking beside the tree-lined river, grand views over the Nidd Valley from the higher points on the route, and a lovely area of woodland near the end. The final stretch is along a gently rising track beside the boundary wall of Ripley Castle, with fine views of both castle and church.

ⓘ Ripley Castle, home of the Ingilby family for nearly 700 years, is an example of a medieval manor house that has been subsequently converted into a comfortable Georgian residence. The fifteenth-century gatehouse, built by

River Nidd near Ripley

Sir John Ingilby, is the oldest part and a fortified tower was added about a century later. The remainder of the castle is basically a late eighteenth-century country house but the three parts – medieval, Tudor and Georgian – all blend together harmoniously. Inside there are fine collections of old books, armour, paintings, china and furniture amassed by several generations of the family. The extensive grounds, comprising a walled garden, lake, waterfalls and deer park, were landscaped by Capability Brown. The nearby church dates mainly from the fourteenth and fifteenth centuries and contains tombs of the Ingilbys. Bullet marks on the east wall are reputed to have been made by Parliamentary soldiers during the execution of Royalist prisoners here following the Battle of Marston Moor in 1644.

While walking around the adjoining estate village, you may be puzzled as to why a relatively small village has a town hall with the French name of Hotel de Ville. The reason is that Sir William Arncotts Ingilby was so impressed with the villages he saw while on a tour of Alsace-Lorraine that he rebuilt Ripley in the French style in the 1820s, complete with town hall, stone cottages and cobbled squares.

❶ **With your back to the Boars Head, walk along the road signposted Car Park. At the traffic island bear right along the A61 in the Harrogate direction (there is a footpath) and where the path bends left, carefully cross the main road and turn right on the other side. Bear left to continue down the parallel former road and cross the bridge over the River Nidd.**

❷ **Turn sharp right along a track, at a public footpath sign, curving left to pass under the main road bridge to a kissing gate. Go through, continue along the right edge of two fields beside the river and in the corner of the second field, follow the path to the left and head gently uphill by the field edge. Turn right over a stile in the top corner, turn left to emerge onto a lane and turn right. From here there are fine views over the Nidd valley. After passing between the buildings of Crag Hill, keep ahead to go through a gate and continue to where the lane bends left.**

❸ **Turn right through a gate, immediately turn left and head diagonally downhill across a field, making for the corner of a hedge and fence. Continue by the hedge and fence on the right to the field corner, where you turn right along the left inside edge of woodland. Turn left over a stile and continue along the right edge of a field, parallel to the River Nidd again. Go through a hedge gap, keep ahead along the right edge of the next field and look out for where you turn right over a waymarked stile. Take the path ahead through trees, cross a footbridge over a stream and turn left along a left field edge by the**

Hampsthwaite church

stream on the left. Continue by the field edge and after passing to the left of a cricket field, you emerge onto a road in Hampsthwaite.

🚶 ❹ **Turn right through the village, passing to the right of the church, and cross the seventeenth-century bridge over the Nidd.**

ℹ Although on an ancient site, Hampsthwaite church was almost entirely rebuilt in the early nineteenth century (apart from the medieval tower) and restored in 1901. It is dedicated to St Thomas à Becket of Canterbury.

🚶 **Continue along the road and where it bends right in front of a row of houses, keep ahead through a gate and head steeply uphill along the right field edge. Continue over the brow and keep ahead to climb a step stile onto a road in the hamlet of Clint. Turn left for a brief detour of about 91 m (100 yards) to take a look at the cross and stocks.**

Looking over Hampsthwaite and the Nidd Valley from Clint

Old cross and stocks in the hamlet of Clint

Above and below: Ripley Castle

Woodland near Ripley

● The old hamlet of Clint, situated high up above the valley, has fine views over Nidderdale. The stocks and base of the old stone cross were renovated in 1977.

⑤ Retrace your steps to where you emerged onto the road and bear left down Hollybank Lane. Follow the lane to where the tarmac ends in front of a house, go through a gate and continue along a track through delightful woodland. On emerging from the trees, Ripley church tower comes into view. Keep along the tree-lined track by the boundary wall of Ripley Castle, heading first down and then up again. On emerging into the village, keep ahead between castle and church to return to the start.

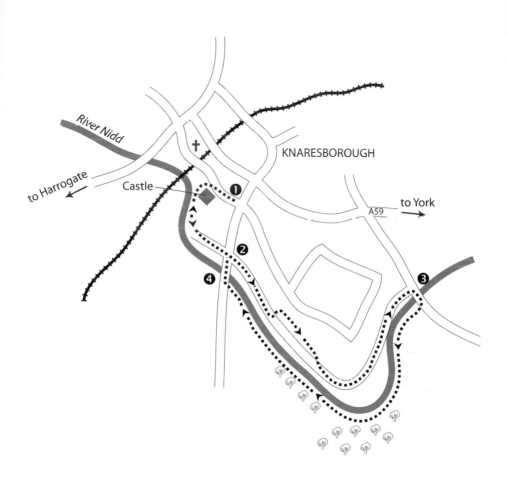

WALK 19

Knaresborough & the River Nidd

....

LENGTH:	6.4 km (4 miles)
TIME:	2 hours
TERRAIN:	Mainly riverside and woodland lanes, tracks and paths; one modest climb
START/PARKING:	Knaresborough, Market Place, GR SE351570. Car parks at Knaresborough
BUS/TRAIN:	Buses from York, Harrogate and Ripon; trains from York and Harrogate
REFRESHMENTS:	Pubs and cafés at Knaresborough
MAP:	*OS Explorer 289 – Leeds*
FROM YORK:	18 miles

....

Considering its modest distance, this is an exceptionally absorbing walk that provides a series of dramatic views, splendid riverside and woodland walking, and plenty of historic interest. From the hilltop town of Knaresborough, with its castle ruins and views over the Nidd, you begin by descending to the river. The rest of the route is beside the river, first walking downstream along its east bank and then returning along the west bank. On the return leg much of the way is through attractive woodland.

❶ With your back to the war memorial and Old Royal Oak Hotel, walk to the end of the market place, passing

Above: Knaresborough Castle
Opposite: the classic view over the Nidd Gorge
from Knaresborough Castle

what claims to be the oldest chemists' shop in the country, in existence since 1720. Turn left, keep ahead through gates, passing to the right of the police station, to enter the grounds of the castle and make your way to the far right-hand corner.

❶ Here is the classic view over the gorge of the River Nidd, spanned by the Victorian railway viaduct, with the houses of the town rising above the river and the tower and spire of the medieval church standing out prominently. Knaresborough Castle, founded by the Normans in the late eleventh century, occupies a commanding position above the Nidd Gorge and surrounding countryside. Most of the surviving remains date from an early fourteenth-century rebuilding, started by Edward I and completed by his son Edward II. The most impressive and complete of these is the mighty keep, or King's Tower. After the Civil War the castle was ordered to be destroyed, a process hastened by the local people who used the castle stones as a cheap source of building material.

Descend a flight of steps, turning sharp left and continuing around more bends down to the riverside promenade. Turn left along it (Waterside) to reach a road to the left of a bridge.

❷ Cross the road, keep ahead along Abbey Road and just after passing a row of cottages, the Chapel of Our Lady of the Crag can be seen to the left.

Situated high above the river, the chapel was carved out of the rock as a wayside shrine in 1408. It is owned by the Roman Catholic Church and services are still held here.

(ⓧ) Continue along a tree-lined track, above the river on the right and at the base of a sheer rock face on the left, and just where the rock face ends – there is a sign here 'Rock Climbing Prohibited' – bear left onto an uphill path. Climb a flight of steps, bend sharp left (doubling back), go up more steps beside the cliff face and at the top turn right onto a level, enclosed path. Keep along it and at a junction of paths and public footpath sign where you emerge into a more open area, keep ahead along the narrower path by a hedge on the right. Continue through woodland above the River Nidd and the path later descends, via steps in places. At the bottom turn left along a tarmac track and soon you pass above St Robert's Cave on the right.

❶ Steps lead down to the cave and to the foundations of a small chapel beside the river, a rare surviving example of the dwelling place of a medieval hermit. St Robert of Knaresborough lived here from about 1180 until his death in 1218, but his aim to lead the secluded life of a hermit was not always possible as his alleged healing powers attracted frequent visitors, including – it is alleged – King John. Even after his death pilgrims continued to come here.

(ⓧ) ❸ On reaching a road, turn right, cross Grimbald Bridge and turn right again along a track. Go through a fence gap, keep ahead along a tarmac track and continue through a caravan park. Beyond the last of the caravans, the route continues along a narrow, tree-lined, undulating riverside path. Keep ahead through another part of the caravan site and turn right, at a yellow-waymarked post, along an enclosed tree-lined path. Now follows a delightful stretch beside the wooded banks of the river. Eventually the path emerges from the trees and continues (fence-lined) across sloping meadows to emerge onto a track at a fork. Take the right-hand waymarked track and

River Nidd near Knaresborough

keep to the left of a gate to continue along an enclosed
path. Keep ahead at a fingerpost, in the direction of
Knaresborough Road Bridge, along a path between walls,
and continue along a track to a road.

❹ Turn right, recross the Nidd and turn left along
Waterside. ❷ Here you pick up the outward route and
either retrace your steps to the start or take any of the
other signed paths on the right which lead back up to
Knaresborough town centre.

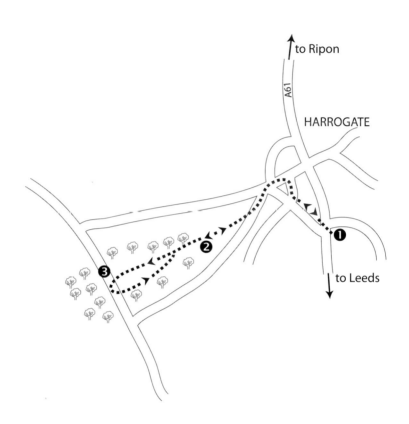

to Ripon

A61

HARROGATE

to Leeds

WALK 20

Harrogate: spa, gardens & woodland

....

LENGTH: 4 km (2.5 miles)

TIME: 1 hour

TERRAIN: Mainly on tarmac and other well-surfaced
               paths through ornamental parkland and
               woodland

START/PARKING: Harrogate, war memorial in Prospect
               Square at the top end of Parliament
               Street, GR SE301553. Car parks at
               Harrogate

BUS/TRAIN: Buses from York, Ripon and Leeds; trains
               from York and Leeds

REFRESHMENTS: Plenty of tea and coffee shops, restaurants,
               wine bars and pubs in Harrogate

MAP: OS Explorer 289 – Leeds

FROM YORK: 20 miles
....

At the start of the walk you pass some of Harrogate's iconic
buildings, erected during the town's heyday as a spa. Then
you enter the beautiful Valley Gardens and continue through
part of an attractive area of woodland on the west side
of the town. This is a short walk which leaves you plenty
of time to appreciate the colourful flower displays in the
gardens and to enjoy an exploration of Harrogate, a most
attractive and distinctive town.

Spring crocuses near the start of the walk in Harrogate

Sun Colonnade, Valley Gardens

ⓘ The starting point overlooks the beautiful, sloping Montpellier Gardens which provide colourful floral displays throughout most of the year. The gardens are at one end of The Stray, an area of over 200 acres of greenery preserved as an area of common land since an act of 1770. It is one of the most distinctive features of Harrogate and possibly looks at its best in early spring when large areas are covered with swathes of crocuses.

❶ From the war memorial, walk down Montpellier Parade, passing Bettys Tea Rooms and at the bottom of the hill follow the road round to the right. Keep to the right of the Crown Hotel to reach a T-junction.

ⓘ Imposing stone Victorian buildings, large green spaces and ornamental gardens all recall Harrogate's heyday as a popular and fashionable spa. Its history as a spa

Pump Room, a reminder of Harrogate's past as a fashionable spa

town began in 1571 when William Slingsby from nearby Knaresborough discovered the first well, allegedly by accident as a result of his horse stumbling. He found that the water had a similar taste and similar properties to that in continental wells, especially those at Spa in Belgium. Later wells were found nearby over the following century and Harrogate developed into a fashionable resort, attracting people from all over the country. It was at its height as a spa in the Victorian and Edwardian period and declined after the First World War. Most of its well-known buildings date from its spa heyday and are situated close to each other.

Just to the right at the T-junction is the Royal Baths, built in 1897. Parts of it are now used as a tourist information centre and a restaurant but it still retains some of its original functions since the Turkish Bath and Health Spa were restored and reopened recently. Across the road is the Royal Hall, opened in 1903 as a spa assembly room.

Above and opposite: Valley Gardens

It was originally called a kursaal, a German word meaning 'cure hall', but for patriotic reasons that name was dropped during World War I. After having been recently restored to its former splendour, it reopened in 1908 and now forms part of Harrogate's International Centre. A short distance to the left is the Pump Room, built in 1842 over the best-known spring in Harrogate, the Old Sulphur Well, reputed to be the strongest sulphur spring in the country. It is now a museum that details the history of Harrogate as a spa. Visitors can sample the sulphurous waters if they wish.

Turn left to the Pump Room and cross the road to enter Valley Gardens. Walk along the main (lower) path and look over to the right to see the impressive Sun Colonnade alongside a parallel higher path. On reaching a circular area where a number of paths meet

Above and below: a winter walk in the Pinewoods

– there is a café on the left – make for a footpath post
and continue along the path signposted to Harlow Car
which heads gently uphill to a three-way fork by another
footpath post.

❶ Valley Gardens occupy land that was once on the edge
of The Stray. The land was bought by the council in 1886
and enlarged to its present size in 1901. Together with the
adjoining Pinewoods, planted in 1796, it extends over 17
acres. The gardens include Bogs Field which contains 36 of
the 88 mineral wells in Harrogate, every one different and
a greater variety of springs than in any other known place.
The Sun Colonnade, which opened in 1933, was originally
a glass-covered walk around 600 feet long and the Sun
Pavilion, at one end of it, was also built in the 1930s. After
being closed for some years, it reopened in 1998.

❷ Take the middle path, signposted to Harlow Car
Gardens, passing between an information board for The
Pinewoods on the left and a war memorial on the right.
Continue through woodland to a road and turn right.

❸ After about 46 m (50 yards), turn right again, at a
public footpath sign, to re-enter the pine woods. The
path continues through the trees, curving slightly right to
reach the war memorial and information board passed
earlier. **❷** Turn left to rejoin the outward route and
retrace your steps through the gardens to return to the
start.

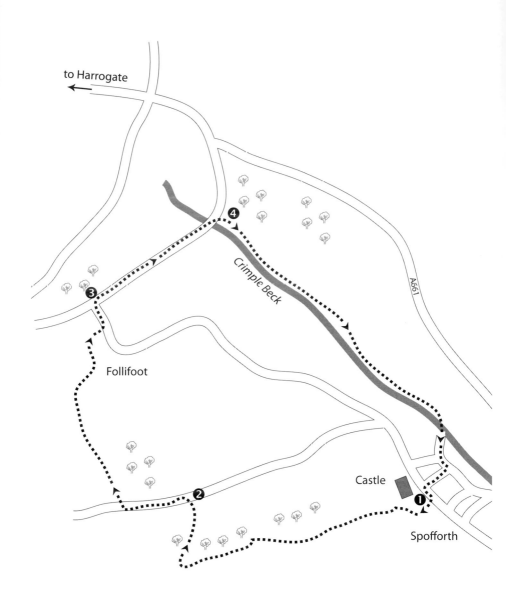

to Harrogate

Crimple Beck

A661

Follifoot

Castle

Spofforth

❶ **❷** **❸** **❹**

WALK 21

Spofforth & Follifoot

....

LENGTH:	8.9 km (5.5 miles)
TIME:	2.5 hours
TERRAIN:	Field paths and tracks across fairly flat terrain
START/PARKING:	Spofforth, on the A661 between Harrogate and Wetherby, GR SE363511, park in the main street near the castle
BUS/TRAIN:	Buses from Harrogate
REFRESHMENTS:	Pubs at Spofforth, pubs at Follifoot
MAP:	OS Explorer 289 – Leeds
FROM YORK:	20 miles

....

This pleasant walk a few miles to the south of Harrogate gives you fine views over gently rolling countryside and plenty of both historic and geological interest. From the castle ruins at Spofforth, well-signed paths and tracks take you to the attractive hilltop village of Follifoot. After a short walk along a road, the remainder of the route is across meadows beside the sparkling little River Crimple. On this final stretch there are views across the fields to the left of the impressive collection of rock formations known as the Spofforth Pinnacles.

ⓘ Despite its name, the ruins of Spofforth Castle are those of a medieval manor house rather than a castle. It was originally built in the late eleventh century and was one of the many homes of the powerful Percy family, earls and later dukes of Northumberland. In 1308 Henry de Percy was allowed to crenellate the house (i.e. to provide it with fortifications) and the surviving buildings, mainly comprising a hall and chamber, date from the fourteenth and fifteenth centuries. Throughout its history Spofforth tended to be neglected as the Percys chiefly concentrated their energies and resources on maintaining the castles at Alnwick and Warkworth, their great strongholds in Northumberland.

❶ **Start in the main street and turn into Manor Garth, passing to the left of the castle. The road becomes first a gravel track and then narrows to a path which passes under a disused railway viaduct and bends right to a gate. Go through and keep ahead along a tree-lined track which curves left and heads gently uphill across a golf course. Where the fence-lined track ends, keep ahead gently downhill and continue along a tree-lined track,**

Spofforth Castle

One of the gatehouses of Rudding Park at Follifoot

eventually turning left to cross a footbridge over a beck. Go through a gate, turn right to walk above the tree-lined bank of the beck and continue along the right edge of two fields. After going through a gate at the end of the second field, turn right along a track. At a junction of tracks just ahead, bear right and the track gradually curves right and heads gently uphill to emerge onto a road.

❷ Turn left – take care, the verges are narrow – and after 400 m (0.25 mile), turn right over a stile, at a public footpath sign, and keep along the right edge of two fields. In the corner of the second field, climb a stile, descend steps to a track, turn left and at a fork immediately ahead, take the right-hand uphill path. The path curves right and continues along the left edge of a field. After following the field edge to the right, turn left through a gap between wall and fence and head gently downhill along the left field edge. Turn right in the bottom corner (still along the left field edge) and follow the broad track as it bends left. The track bends left again and later bends right, passing between houses to emerge onto a road. Turn left into Follifoot and turn left again along the main street up to a T-junction by the war memorial and in front of one of the gatehouses of Rudding Park.

❶ From the pleasant hilltop village of Follifoot there are extensive views across the Vale of York. The village is dominated by the south gatehouse of Rudding Park, once a large country estate. The great house, built in the early nineteenth century, is now a luxury hotel, conference centre and golfing resort. A short distance down the road to the right you pass the small Victorian village church.

❸ Turn right along Plompton Road and keep along it for 1.2 km (0.75 miles) – there are verges both sides but take care.

❹ Immediately after crossing the bridge over Crimple Beck (or River Crimple) turn right, at a public footpath sign, and climb a stile. Turn right and continue along the right edge of a series of fields and over a succession of stiles, following the twists and turns of the small river.

❶ Over to the left you get fine views of a group of dramatic gritstone boulders called the Spofforth Pinnacles, an extension of the nearby Plumpton Rocks. Their fantastic shapes are the result of weathering over the centuries.

When you see a footbridge over the river, turn right over it and the path bends left and continues between fences

Spofforth Pinnacles

towards a former mill. Turn right over another footbridge, turn left along a walled tarmac path, go through a squeezer stile and walk along a lane into Spofforth. At a crossroads, keep ahead along Beech Lane which leads to a T-junction in front of the castle and turn left to the start.

Crimple Beck near Spofforth

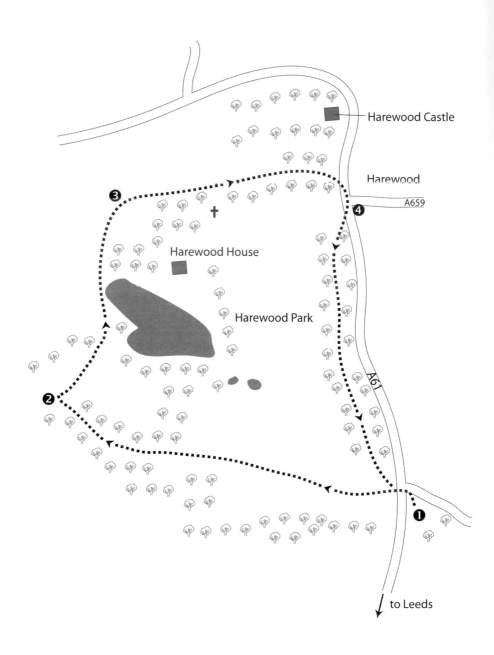

Harewood Castle

Harewood

A659

Harewood House

Harewood Park

A61

to Leeds

WALK 22

Harewood House & Park

....

LENGTH:	8 km (5 miles)
TIME:	2.5 hours
TERRAIN:	Well-signposted route mainly across undulating parkland and through woods
START/PARKING:	Harewood, parking spaces at the junction of the A61 and the lane signposted to Wike about 1.25 miles south of Harewood village, GR SE326432
BUS/TRAIN:	Buses from Leeds and Harrogate to Harewood village from where you could pick up the walk at point 4
REFRESHMENTS:	Pub at Harewood, cafés at Harewood House
MAP:	*OS Explorer 289 – Leeds*
FROM YORK:	25 miles

....

The line of the route is square-shaped, an 'across, up, across and down' walk that basically follows the perimeter of Harewood Park. The park is a mixture of open grassland and woodland and right from the start there are fine views across to the imposing façade of Harewood House. The house, church, nearby ruined castle and village all contribute to an understanding of the evolution of a country estate and a visit to the great house, probably best after completing the walk, is definitely recommended.

Above and below: landscaped parkland at Harewood

Opposite: Harewood House

(🚶) ❶ Begin by crossing the A61 to a public bridleway sign and go through gates to enter the Harewood Estate. As you walk along a track, fine distant views open up to the right looking across the park to Harewood House.

ⓘ Harewood House is one of the grandest of England's country houses and reflects the wealth of the Lascelles family who acquired the estate in 1738. Construction of the house was begun by Edwin Lascelles in 1759 and a list of some of the people who worked on it reads like a roll call of the greatest names of the day. John Carr was the architect, the interior was designed by Robert Adam, Thomas Chippendale (a local man from Otley) made the furniture and Capability Brown was responsible for the landscaping of the park. Apart from some nineteenth-century changes by architect Charles Barry (he gave the house a more Italianate look and added the terrace)

Harewood remains much the same as when it was completed in the late eighteenth century. The tour of the house comprises the state rooms on the ground floor, which include bedrooms, sitting rooms, three libraries, music room, gallery and dining room, and you can also go 'below stairs' and get some idea of how the servants lived. The state rooms possess many fine paintings, porcelain and – as might be expected – one of the greatest collections of Chippendale furniture in the country. As you walk around the formal terrace gardens, or perhaps sample a cream tea from the Terrace Café, you can enjoy the grand views across the lake and over the extensive parkland through which you have walked.

Ⓧ **The track gently descends to a gate. Go through, continue through woodland and as you cross a bridge over a stream, look to the left for an attractive view of a cascade. At a T-junction immediately in front, turn left and the track curves right to a fork. Take the right-hand track which continues through the trees, and at a fingerpost turn right and head down to a junction of tracks. At a fork ahead, take the right hand-track which heads downhill to a T-junction and turn right.**

Ⓧ ❷ **Walk gently downhill, bear left at a public bridleway sign and continue down to the bottom. Keep ahead by woodland on the left, enjoying a view of the lake to the right and the house perched above it, to a T-junction. Turn left and the track bends right to a gate. Go through, head gently uphill by a wall on the right, curving left to join and continue along a tarmac track. Descend quite steeply and at a fork at the bottom, take the left-hand track. Cross a bridge, continue up to a gate, go through and head up to go through two more gates to the top. Keep ahead to a T-junction and footpath sign. Ahead is a grand view over the Wharfe valley.**

Formal gardens at Harewood House

View over the park from the terrace garden

(🚶) ❸ **Turn right along a tarmac track which continues to climb by a wall on the right, later levelling off. After going through a gate, the route continues ahead but a brief detour along the walled track on the right brings you to Harewood church.**

❶ Harewood church occupies an isolated position on the edge of the park. This is because when the house was built and the park landscaped, the original village was demolished and a new one – the present village – was built by the main entrance to the park. The village – like the house – was built by John Carr and has a uniformity of design, as will be seen shortly when you reach it. Harewood Castle, the predecessor of the house, is a fourteenth-century ruin situated just off the A61 to the north of the village. It is not open to the public but can be glimpsed from the main road.

The church was built in the early fifteenth century and redesigned at the time of the building of the house in the late eighteenth century. It is particularly noted for having one of the finest collections of alabaster tombs and monuments in the country. These are for the various families that owned the Harewood estate during the fifteenth and early sixteenth centuries. Nowadays the church is not used for regular worship and is maintained by the Churches Conservation Trust.

(🚶) **Return to the main route, continue along the track, go through a gate and keep ahead into Harewood village. Turn right at the main road and just beyond the main entrance to the park and house, look out for a gate in the wall on the right which has a sign 'Wallside Permissive Path Entrance'.**

(🚶) ❹ **Go through the gate and up some steps and take the path ahead through the trees, bending right to a**

T-junction. Turn left and continue along a track through woodland for 1.6 km (1 mile). After emerging from the trees, keep ahead through two gates to a T-junction. Turn left, go through the gates of the park and cross the A61 to return to the start.

Looking over the Wharfe valley near Harewood

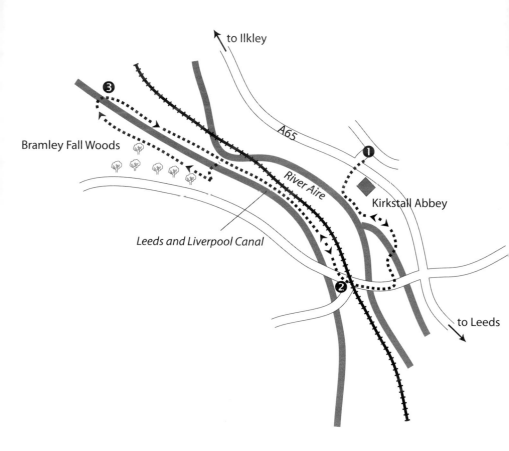

to Ilkley

A65

River Aire

3

Bramley Fall Woods

1

Kirkstall Abbey

Leeds and Liverpool Canal

2

to Leeds

WALK 23

Kirkstall Abbey & the Leeds & Liverpool Canal

....

LENGTH:	6.4 km (4 miles)
TIME:	2 hours
TERRAIN:	Easy walking on well-surfaced park, woodland and canalside paths
START/PARKING:	Kirkstall Valley Park, off A65 2.5 miles north west of Leeds city centre, GR SE260364
BUS/TRAIN:	Buses from Leeds city centre
REFRESHMENTS:	Pubs at Kirkstall, café at Abbey House Museum
MAPS:	*OS Explorers 289 – Leeds* and *288 – Bradford & Huddersfield*
FROM YORK:	27 miles

....

In places this walk has such a rural feel to it – quiet waterways, woodland paths and views across fields – that it is difficult to believe that you are scarcely more than 2 miles from the centre of Leeds and close to busy roads and motorways. This is because it is based on the Kirkstall Valley Park, part of the West Leeds Country Park and Green Gateways, an ambitious project to create a green corridor stretching along the Aire valley from the city centre out to the western suburbs and the countryside beyond. The walk starts in parkland by the splendid ruins of Kirkstall Abbey and much

of it is along the peaceful towpath of the Leeds and Liverpool
Canal and through the attractive Bramley Fall Woods.

ⓘ Situated close to a main road in a suburban park on the
edge of Leeds, Kirkstall obviously lacks the rural seclusion
of some of the other great abbeys of Yorkshire (Fountains,
Rievaulx and Byland) but nevertheless has an attractive
location on the banks of the River Aire and ranks as one
of the best-preserved monastic ruins in the country. It
was founded by the Cistercians in 1147 and most of it
dates from the second half of the twelfth century. After
its dissolution in 1539, the abbey passed through several
hands until being donated to the city of Leeds in the late
nineteenth century. Following necessary restoration work, it
opened to the public in 1895.

Given its location in a highly urbanised area, it is
surprising that it has managed to survive at all. Although
the A65 separates it from the former gatehouse – now the
Abbey House Museum – in the early nineteenth century
the main road into Leeds actually ran through the middle
of the nave. In spite of this, the remains are both extensive
and impressive and merit a thorough exploration. The
church, a superb example of Norman architecture, stands
to its full height and retains part of its central tower, and
the remains of the domestic buildings grouped around the
cloister are unusually complete. A new development is a
visitor centre which is housed in the reredorter, the former
toilet area of the monastery.

Across the road housed in the monastic gatehouse is
the Abbey House Museum, also well worth a visit. There
are childhood and costume galleries and reconstructed
Victorian streets to explore, showing what life was like in
nineteenth-century Leeds.

🚶 ❶ Begin by crossing the main road to enter the abbey
grounds and take the tarmac path that passes the west

The imposing ruins of Kirkstall Abbey

Abbey House Museum, Kirkstall

River Aire at Kirkstall

front of the church and bears right in front of the visitor centre to a T-junction. Turn left alongside the south side of the ruins and just before reaching a gate, turn right onto a path parallel to the main road on the left and above the River Aire on the right. At the next fork take the right-hand path, heading downhill and curving right to cross a footbridge over an arm of the river. The path then bears left through trees to a road. Turn right, cross Kirkstall Bridge over the Aire and railway line, and at a fork take the left-hand road. Cross Wyther Lane, walk across grass to the canal and turn right onto the towpath.

ⓘ It was in order to link Leeds and the woollen towns of Yorkshire with the port of Liverpool that the Leeds and Liverpool Canal was built. Construction began in the late eighteenth century and the canal was completed in 1816, making it the equivalent of the M62 at the time. Its total length is just over 127 miles, the longest single canal in Britain.

Leeds and Liverpool Canal near Kirkstall

(🕊) ❷ Keep alongside the canal for the next 1.2 km (0.75 miles) to Forge Locks. At the top lock, climb steps and turn left to cross a footbridge over the canal. Keep ahead up a flight of steps through woodland and at the top, turn right along a path signposted Canalside Walk. The next part of the walk is particularly pleasant as the path continues through Bramley Fall Woods, with the canal below on the right and fine views across the Aire valley. At a fingerpost near the next group of locks (Newlay Locks), turn right and recross the canal via a footbridge.

(🕊) ❸ Turn right onto the towpath and follow the canal back to Forge Locks. Here you pick up the outward route and retrace your steps to the start.

Bramley Fall Woods near Kirkstall

The west front of Kirkstall Abbey

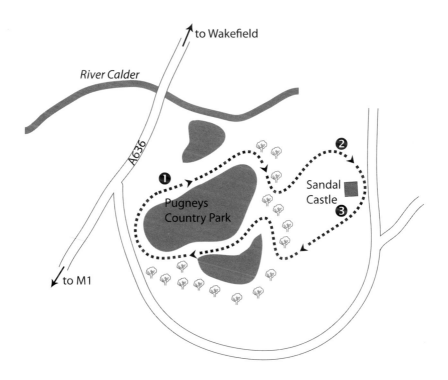

WALK 24

Pugneys Country Park & Sandal Castle

....

LENGTH:	4.8 km (3 miles)
TIME:	1.5 hours
TERRAIN:	Easy and well-surfaced paths, one modest climb and descent
START/PARKING:	Pugneys Country Park, off A636 2 miles south west of Wakefield city centre, GR SE325180
BUS/TRAIN:	Buses from Wakefield city centre
REFRESHMENTS:	Pub by the entrance to Pugneys Country Park, café at the country park
MAP:	OS Explorer 278 – Sheffield & Barnsley
FROM YORK:	32 miles

....

The first and last parts of the walk are beside a lake, with fine views across the water dominated by the dramatic-looking ruins of Sandal Castle on the skyline. The middle section of the walk consists of a steady climb up to the castle, followed by a descent. The climb is worth it because the magnificent all-round views from the castle extend across the site of the Battle of Wakefield to the buildings in the city centre, including the tower and spire of Wakefield Cathedral.

Above and opposite: Sandal Castle

ⓘ The 250-acre Pugneys Country Park is a fine example of how derelict industrial eyesores can be made both useful and attractive. It opened in 1985 on the sites of a former open cast coal mine and gravel and sand quarry and comprises two lakes, surrounding grassland and woodland. The larger of the lakes is encircled by a well-surfaced path and is used for watersports, the smaller one is a nature reserve. Overlooking the country park are the scanty but dramatic ruins of Sandal Castle.

⚐ ❶ Walk to the far end of the car park and keep ahead along the lakeside path, curving right following the shore of the lake. On a right bend just after passing to the right of a group of trees, turn left, at a sign 'Pathway to Sandal Castle', onto a narrower path and cross a footbridge. Turn right, almost immediately turn left and head uphill towards the castle remains. At a T-junction turn left and continue gently uphill along an enclosed path.

(🚶) ❷ **Look out for where you turn sharp right and continue up across fields, finally emerging onto a road. Turn right and right again at the entrance to Sandal Castle and Visitor Centre.**

ⓘ The disappearance of most of the stonework at Sandal Castle has one advantage: it reveals the impressive earthworks which enable visitors to appreciate the plan of a typical motte and bailey castle. The original earth and timber castle was founded in the early twelfth century and was rebuilt and strengthened with stone defences, mostly during the thirteenth century. The motte, or mound, supported a stone keep, of which only a few foundations remain. The most important event in the castle's history

A view of Sandal Castle

Overlooking the site of the Battle of Wakefield

came during the Wars of the Roses when it was the setting for the Battle of Wakefield in 1460. It seems to have subsequently fallen into decay during the Tudor period but was briefly reoccupied during the Civil War in the 1640s. Afterwards it was slighted, i.e. stripped of its fortifications, and fell into ruin. Finds revealed by excavation can be seen in the visitor centre.

The site of the Battle of Wakefield, fought between Lancastrians and Yorkists on 30 December 1460, lies between the castle and centre of Wakefield and can be seen from the castle mound. Sandal Castle was one of the strongholds of Richard Duke of York and in December 1460 a Lancastrian army marched from Pontefract and laid siege to it. Instead of staying in the comparative safety of the castle while he waited for reinforcements, Richard

Pugneys Country Park

attacked the Lancastrians, possibly believing that their forces were smaller than they were, and attempted to drive them towards the River Calder. He was taken by surprise as additional enemy troops who had been concealed by woodland emerged from the trees and joined in the battle. Despite fighting bravely, the Yorkists, outnumbered and surrounded, were heavily defeated and were pursued by the victorious Lancastrians towards Wakefield, where many were slain. Richard himself was killed in the battle and his head was subsequently displayed on Micklegate Bar in York. Within a year, however, the tables had been turned and his son had become King Edward IV.

❸ **Walk across to the castle mound and turn left along the path that encircles it. Where this path bends right by a bench, turn left and head down to a stile. After climbing it, keep ahead along the top left edge of a field heading gently downhill, and at a T-junction turn right and continue downhill along the left field edge. In the bottom corner turn left over a plank footbridge and turn right along the right edge of the next field. Climb a stile onto a track, turn right and almost immediately turn left alongside farm buildings. Keep ahead, cross a footbridge over Pugneys Drain to a T-junction and turn right. Follow the path around a left bend and at another T-junction in front of the lake, turn left. Follow the lakeside path as it curves right to return to the start.**

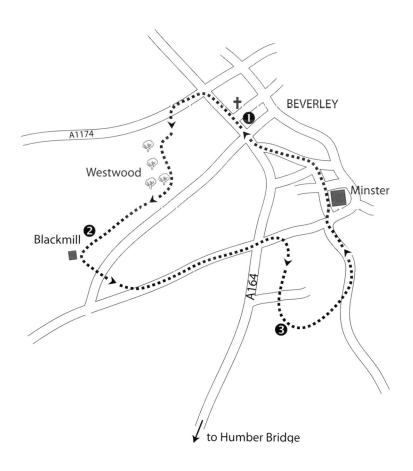

WALK 25

Around Beverley

....

LENGTH:	6.4 km (4 miles)
TIME:	2 hours
TERRAIN:	Easy walking along roads and footpaths and across grassland
START/PARKING:	Beverley, Saturday Market, GR TA033397. Plenty of car parks at Beverley
BUS/TRAIN:	Buses from York and Hull; trains from Hull
REFRESHMENTS:	Plenty of pubs, cafes, wine bars and coffee shops at Beverley
MAP:	*OS Explorer 293 – Kingston upon Hull & Beverley*
FROM YORK:	30 miles

....

This is a walk that combines the best of town and country,
all in a surprisingly modest distance. A few minutes after
leaving the town centre, you emerge onto the open grassy
expanses of Westwood, one of a number of commons that
have been retained around the edge of Beverley. From
here the many grand views are inevitably dominated by
the towers of the minster. The route continues around the
western and southern fringes of the town and the final
stretch brings more memorable views of the minster and a
walk through the historic heart of Beverley.

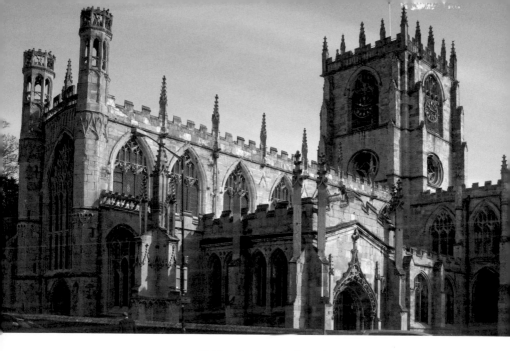

St Mary's church, Beverley

ⓘ The fact that Beverley has not one but two magnificent medieval churches – either of which could pass for a cathedral – is a testament to the town's prosperity in the Middle Ages. This prosperity was based on the production of brick, leather and especially a flourishing woollen industry. The town was also an important market centre.

One of these churches, St Mary's, is situated near the start of the walk. This large cruciform church dates from the twelfth century but was extensively rebuilt and extended in the late fourteenth and fifteenth centuries during the heyday of the woollen trade. Both in the scale and quality of its architecture it resembles the well-known 'wool churches' of the Cotswolds. Particularly outstanding are the west front, choir stalls and central tower. The latter, constructed in the fifteenth century, collapsed in 1520 causing the death of many worshippers. It was quickly rebuilt and the church was thoroughly restored in the nineteenth century.

① The walk starts by the eighteenth-century market cross in Saturday Market. Walk along North Bar Within, passing St Mary's church on the right, and go through North Bar into North Bar Without.

North Bar was built in the early fifteenth century and is the finest example in England of a brick-built town gate. Medieval Beverley was never defended by stone walls but was surrounded by a ditch and earth ramparts and originally had four gates, or bars. This is the only one to survive.

Turn left along York Road, and soon you emerge onto the open expanses of Westwood Common. Where the road bears right, bear left onto a tarmac path that heads diagonally across the grass towards trees. The path curves left and heads gently uphill through the trees to emerge into an open area again. Turn right and head across the grass by the edge of the woodland on the right and continue across the common to Blackmill, the prominent disused windmill seen on the horizon.

Westwood is the largest of a number of areas of common pasture that have survived around the edge of Beverley, and the northern part of it houses the race course. There were once several windmills dotted around the common and Blackmill (last used in the 1860s) is the most conspicuous and best-preserved of these.

② At the windmill turn left and walk in a straight line to a road. Cross over, continue across the common to the next road and to the left are fine views of the towers of the minster. Over to the right another windmill can be seen, incorporated into the club house of the golf club. Turn left, walk beside the road, and at the end of the common continue along the road (Cartwright Lane) back into the town. Keep ahead at a crossroads and turn right

along Kitchen Lane – there is a cycleway sign here. Pass to the left of some allotments and keep ahead where the lane narrows to an enclosed track. Follow the track around a right bend and just before emerging onto a road, turn left along a tarmac track. After the tarmac ends, continue along a stony, hedge-lined track which emerges onto a road. Cross over, keep ahead along a tarmac track and after crossing another track the way continues along a narrow, enclosed path. Go up steps and keep ahead along a tarmac path to a junction of paths by a small triangular patch of grass.

(𝕏) ❸ Turn left through a kissing gate and walk along a path, by a stream on the left, which soon widens into a track. To the left are views of the south side of Beverley Minster. On reaching a lane, turn left and follow it around a left bend to a road junction by the minster.

Beverley Minster

View over Beverley from Westwood

If you thought St Mary's church was impressive, Beverley Minster is guaranteed to take your breath away. It is widely regarded as the finest non-cathedral church in the country and in the Middle Ages served as a sub-cathedral for the vast diocese of York. The church was founded in the seventh century by John, Bishop of York, who retired to Beverley. He was later canonised and throughout the medieval period the shrine of St John of Beverley was a major centre of pilgrimage. The present church, a masterpiece of Gothic architecture, was begun in 1220 and completed about 200 years later. The west front is particularly elaborate and the interior is noted for the elegant soaring arches in the nave and choir.

Keep ahead along St John Street, passing the west front of the minster, and turn right at a T-junction. Turn left along Highgate which emerges into Wednesday Market and keep ahead, first along Butcher Row and then Toll Gavel to return to the starting point in Saturday Market.

Also available from Carnegie Publishing

*Visit **www.carnegiepublishing.com** for our full catalogue and pricing information.*

DISCOUNTS AVAILABLE ONLINE

Birdwatching walks in the Yorkshire Dales

by Brendan Threlfall

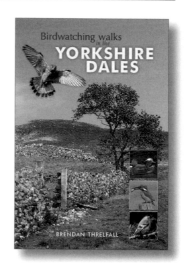

Pages: 192, softback
Illustrations: maps & colour photos
Page size: 234 × 156 mm
ISBN: 978-1-874181-53-8
Price: £7.95

The Yorkshire Dales is an enchantingly beautiful area in the heart of northern England. It is a land of limestone pavements and scars, fast-flowing rivers and dramatic waterfalls, lonely heather moors and picturesque villages and valleys. But as well as its wonderful landscapes, the Dales is also a special place for many bird species, and these twin assets are combined in this excellent new book. Each of these well designed walks is set in gorgeous countryside where there is also every chance of seeing some of the birds which abounds in the area. Both novice and experienced birders can enjoy the dippers at Aysgarth, or great spotted woodpeckers in Grass Woods, as well as the rarer black grouse, wood warbler, pied flycatcher and nightjar, to name but a few.

With helpful guide maps, interesting bird and habitat information, travel hints and a bird reference section, Birdwatching walks in the Yorkshire Dales should ensure that walkers of all abilities really can get the best out of this stunning National Park and its rich and varied bird population.

A history of Yorkshire: 'County of the Broad Acres'

by Prof. David Hey

Pages: 480, hardback
Illustrations: 495, mostly in full colour
Page size: 243 × 169 mm
ISBN: 978-1-85936-122-1
Price: £24

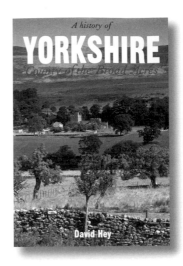

"A Triumph of Local History Writing"

"This book is magnificent (there is no other word for it), fitting both in scale and quality its subject. Ranging from the Stone Age to the 1990s, it is no mean feat to have captured in 140,000 words the essential history of a county that comprises almost one-eighth of England. David Hey, however, rises to the challenge with a bravura performance that sets a new standard for popular county and regional histories. The book is also visually ravishing. Hey's text is graced by around 500 carefully chosen illustrations, many of them high-definition colour photographs specially taken for the volume ... "

(Prof. Malcolm Chase, University of Leeds)

The history of Yorkshire is more varied than that of any other English county. The changing fortunes of the many different regions of the county – from Pennine moors and valley towns to the flats of Holderness; from industrialised cities to quiet market towns – are a major theme in David Hey's acclaimed masterpiece.

More from our *Historic walks* series by Brian Conduit

These excellent books guide walkers of all abilities around both city and country in a series of 25 well-thought-out routes, each accompanied by a helpful map, historical background information and photographs. **Brian Conduit** is a much-published walk author whose experience and knowledge of each area will be obvious to all who use these beautifully produced books.

Newcastle-upon-Tyne is one of the most visually exciting cities in Britain. It is one of the few to possess a medieval castle, while handsome and dignified classical buildings grace its centre, as well as some stunning examples of modern architecture.

Birmingham is a city of contrasts. Although it still bears some of the scars of its industrial past, in recent years it has been transformed through a series of impressive modern developments, while at the same time conserving and enhancing its remaining Victorian buildings. With its attractively restored canals and rejuvenated centre it is now a very pleasant and interesting place to explore. But the city also has the advantage of lying at the heart of some of the most beautiful and varied countryside in England.

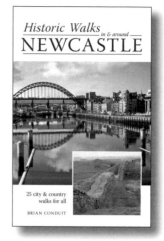

Historic Walks in & around
NEWCASTLE

25 city & country walks for all

BRIAN CONDUIT

Pages: 192, softback
Illust.: maps, colour photos
Page size: 216 × 138 mm
ISBN: 978-1-874181-52-1
Price: £8.95

Historic Walks in & around
BIRMINGHAM

25 city & country walks for all

BRIAN CONDUIT

Pages: 192, softback
Illust.: maps, colour photos
Page size: 216 × 138 mm
ISBN: 978-1-874181-51-4
Price: £8.95